WALKING IN
TWO WORLDS

WALKING IN TWO WORLDS

WAB KINEW

PENGUIN TEEN

an imprint of Penguin Random House Canada Young Readers,
a division of Penguin Random House of Canada Limited

Published in hardcover by Penguin Teen, 2021

1 2 3 4 5 6 7 8 9 10

Manufactured in Canada

LIBRARY AND ARCHIVES CANADA CATALOGUING IN PUBLICATION

Title: Walking in two worlds / Wab Kinew.
Names: Kinew, Wab, 1981- author.
Identifiers: Canadiana (print) 20200399373 | Canadiana (ebook) 20200399411
| ISBN 9780735269002 (hardcover) | ISBN 9780735269019 (EPUB)
Classification: LCC PS8621.I54 W35 2021 | DDC jC813/.6—dc23

Library of Congress Control Number: 2020950733

www.penguinrandomhouse.ca

Penguin
Random House
PENGUIN TEEN CANADA

To the students at
Pelican Falls First Nations High School:

Visiting your school over the years,
I've noticed you face many things going to
school away from home, some good and some bad,
but you face them all with courage.

I started this book thinking it might be cool if you
could read something that represented our backgrounds
and some of the realities you face.

Ando-bawaajigek—seek your dreams!

"We don't want to create two worlds, but walk together in one world—relating to each other as having our own uniqueness that we mutually respect."

—SENATOR MURRAY SINCLAIR

Anishinaabe Terms and Pronunciation Guide

Anama'edaa (*ah-numb-ah-yay-TAH*): Let us pray

Anishinaabe (*a-nish-in-NAH-bay*): Ojibwe or Indigenous

Bagonegiizhigok (*bug-oh-nay-KEESH-ig-oak*): Hole in the day

Baakinan (*buck-in-NONE*): Open it!

Binesi (*bin-NEH-see*): Thunderbird

Eniwek igo kiga'onji-pimaadiz ndiwe'igan (*AY-knee-wake EE-go key-gohn-jih-pee-MAH-tizz in-tay-WAY-gun*): Through my drum you will live just that much more

Kookom (*COOK-em*): Grandmother

Mishi-pizhiw (*mi-SHIP-i-shoe*): A supernatural being in Anishinaabe culture

Nameg (*nah-MAYK*): Sturgeon (plural)

Ni-noonde-pimaadiz (*nih-known-day-pee-MAH-tizz*): I want to live

Onizhishin Anishinaabe Aking (*oh-NISH-ish-in ah-nish-in-NAW-bay AH-king*): Anishinaabe country is beautiful

Onjine (*OWN-jin-nay*): The way you behave will come back to you

Patai'itiwin (*put-TIE-it-tee-win*): The way you behave will come back to your children

Waawaate (*WAH-wah-tay*): The northern lights

CHAPTER 1

It was the best of Bugz, it was the worst of Bugz. She created life, she destroyed worlds. She appeared invincible, she knew only defeat. She was Indigenous, she didn't belong. She moved with absolute confidence, she couldn't shake the tiny voice inside: *It's no big deal, it's the end of the world.* In many ways, Bugz was just like everybody else . . . until she went online into the Floraverse. There, Bugz's every move was watched by the entire world, who either loved her or hated her.

Hidden by total darkness, Bugz pressed her body close to a cedar tree, edging nearer to danger. She rarely hid in the virtual world of the 'Verse. Apart from her celebrity, there was her look: she wore a custom skin with an athletic physique packed into a black, neon-pink, and Day-Glo-green outfit. The ensemble borrowed from the body armor of science-fiction superheroes and the embroidered designs of a pow-wow dancer. Floral patterns that paid homage to the beadwork of her Anishinaabe Ancestors accented her bodysuit. Her midriff was exposed in a way that would've raised eyebrows among the aunties back on the Rez. Those older women preached modesty, but anytime Bugz's mom heard those so-called teachings that singled out women's bodies, she'd always stick up for her daughter and say, "That's just the colonization talking."

Bugz tossed her hair to one side and leaned in closer to her prey. Her heads-up-display visor cast a rose-colored glow across her cheekbones as she studied her targets. On-screen, a stream of comments flooded her peripheral vision. She paid the chat feed absolutely no mind, at least not for the moment. Her vision narrowed to a tunnel as she prepared for a huge battle, one she had no intention of losing. Besides, she'd turned her location off hours ago so no one on the stream could reveal her plan to the marks. She inched closer to the edge of the cedar trees and listened to them shouting down below. All five hundred of them. She liked her odds.

"We worked too hard and fought too long for anything less than victory!"

Bugz recognized the imposing eight-foot-tall warrior now shouting—Alpha. A scar bisected his face, testifying to a past battle. His eyes—each a different color, one green and one brown—reminded Bugz of a wild dog, a husky that fled captivity and returned as the leader of a pack of wolves. Bugz knew his online backstory. Alpha began his ascent in the 'Verse by slaughtering the gamer clan that welcomed him in as a noob. As fierce as he looked he still only stood second in the 'Verse's global fan rankings. Bugz slowly drew a deep breath and reminded herself that she ranked #1.

Bugz noted all of Alpha's followers gathered below wore an Ø symbol on their arms as a way of paying homage to their scarred leader. They called themselves Clan:LESS, the clan that was not a clan, a nod to Alpha cannibalizing his first team. They counted among their ranks a mishmash of the best soldiers and mercenaries from across the Floraverse. Bugz studied their artillery: massive guns, laser cannons, and the coolest energy swords crypto could buy. *Not bad,* she thought to herself. *But nothing special.*

"For years we've journeyed across the 'Verse seeking what is rightfully ours!" Alpha yelled. Bugz, still hidden, rolled her eyes. "The resources, the creatures, the weapons we need to dominate the Spirit World. All of it is rightfully ours. Men built this technology, men perfected the blockchain, and now it's run by a woman? No! We will take it back from *her.*" Bugz studied Alpha, scanning the obedient stares of his charges. "We'll take it back in battle. She can never beat us . . . we must always win!" The crowd roared its approval.

Gross. Bugz stepped farther back behind the cedar tree. She hated Clan:LESS—they harassed women who played the game, shared sexist content, and banned women from joining their ranks.

"I thought this VR and AR stuff promised to make a *better* world," Bugz whispered to herself. The chat in her display screen exploded with comments. "Oh well. I guess we can create better technology without becoming better people."

She peeked around the corner of her hiding spot again and sized up the battlefield. At present, 499 Clan:LESS members encircled Alpha, still hanging on his every word. He screamed at the assembled troops, psyching them up for the coming battle.

"This coward Bugz wants to take your lives from you. She wants to take your weapons from you. She wants to force you to respawn and lose everything you've fought for." Alpha paused for dramatic effect. "But will you let that happen?"

"NO!" roared the crowd.

"Are we going to fight?!" Alpha shouted.

"YES!" the crowd replied.

"Are we going to win?"

"YES!"

"We launch our sneak attack tonight!" concluded Alpha, thrusting his fist in the air.

"YEAHHH!" The crowd responded by punching their weapons into the sky and high-fiving the clanmates closest to them. They chanted Alpha's name.

"Pro tip: don't announce your sneak attack before you actually launch your sneak attack." Bugz winked to her audience streaming along online. Millions of her followers watched from their own heads-up displays inside the 'Verse or on phones in the real world. Bugz crouched, bending her knees, as she prepared to leap out from her hiding spot. She felt a bead of sweat gathering on her brow in real life. The chat in her display sparkled with activity.

"Ahh, what am I getting all tensed up for?" She blew her hair away quickly, stood up straight, and stepped out of the shadows. "Hey losers, look over here!"

Some of Bugz's viewers were warning the Clan:LESS horde an attack was imminent. The warriors who noticed the warnings took their eyes off Alpha and began scanning the horizon. They were the first to see her. Bugz—the specter, the legend, the phenom—appeared before them, all swagger and attitude. She pulled a flaming, torch-tipped spear back like a javelin thrower, illuminating her bodysuit in the process. She took careful aim and launched the projectile in a long, soaring arc that delivered its payload directly to the center of the crowd. She stood on one leg to admire her throw as the spear landed, splattering the horde of Clan:LESS soldiers with fire and flame.

Instantly dozens of soldiers evaporated into the ether.

"S3reum was eliminated by Bugz."

"Nigel_The_Knight was eliminated by Bugz."

"xx.GFguerilla.xx was eliminated by Bugz."

Dozens of other gamertags flickered and disappeared into the sky.

The wounded stampeded in all directions.

"You cowards!" Alpha cried. "Don't run! This is what we wanted. Our enemy is right here. The battle is on!"

Bugz stood on the higher ground, taking in the carnage and confusion below and feeling quite proud of herself. She looked down to see one member of Clan:LESS just staring at her, frozen. She laughed. Bugz got this sort of reaction all the time. Other gamers often seized up in her presence like kids meeting a childhood idol.

"Get her!" Alpha yelled. The 450 or so surviving members of Clan:LESS tore up the incline as Bugz turned to the hills and ran.

Before she could reach a full sprint, laser beams and machine-gun fire rained down all around. As if dodging the spray from one gun wasn't hard enough, Bugz found herself dodging overlapping fire from several automatic weapons at once. She moved as though she had the power to slow down time. As the tsunami of weapon fire chased her, she bobbed and weaved a perfect path that avoided each beam and bullet.

With so much firepower bearing down, there came a moment when no path remained for Bugz, no way to move that wouldn't see her riddled with slugs and lasers. In this instant, the chat screen in her heads-up display filled with expletives and shouting.

"d@rcy987: INCOMING!"

"sweet_n_lowa: #!@& no!"

"Porselyn: Holy @#$%!"

The Floraverse's automatic chat-censoring captured

the worry of the fans watching Bugz's livestream. They all aspired to fight as forcefully and move as gracefully themselves, but none could match Bugz's preternatural ability in the 'Verse. So they watched her, imagining themselves in her shoes. Or moccasins.

The view counter ticked upward; this battle between the Floraverse's greatest individual warrior and the most ruthless clan in existence was pulling in the most views in the history of the game. But with the artillery closing in, it seemed as though it would come to a premature end. In just a millisecond, the lasers, bullets, and spears would converge on Bugz and eviscerate her.

But just as the first of the beams approached, Bugz traced a quick zigzag motion through the air behind her. Instantly the roots of the nearby trees tore through the earth and grew thick, forming a shield. The laser beams and gunfire ripped through this organic barrier in a fraction of a second, but Bugz didn't need any more than that. By the time the gunfire obliterated the plant matter, Bugz had gained a step and was once again weaving a perfect path through the mayhem.

Her chat screen exploded with gold coins, flowers, and diamond rings as her fans showered her with gifts, inspired by her virtuosity. Bugz could back herself into a corner and stun them all with an impossible escape. Fans paid for the virtual gifts themselves with real money or crypto, and Bugz, like everyone else in the Floraverse who received a gift, earned a micropayment every time she received something from a fan. Bugz glanced at her balance. She'd just earned enough to buy a new car.

Behind her, Alpha raised a giant, oversized cannon onto his shoulder. It resembled a jet engine, with a blue-and-white glow sparking outward from where the turbine should have been. He aimed and fired a massive energy blast, incinerating a huge chunk of the forest and splattering shrapnel up the hillside toward Bugz.

As the explosion closed in on Bugz, the heavens opened up and what looked like a giant black eagle screamed down from the sky. It swooped down to Bugz, snatched her in its talons, and lifted her up to the clouds. Another energy blast tore a huge chunk out of the mountainside and triggered an avalanche. This buried the first lines of Clan:LESS warriors on the hill and sent the others running back down the slope until the rockslide abated.

Bugz rode the Thunderbird over the peak of the mountain.

"Monff: HOW are you so lucky?"

"BhadBhab: Nice save!"

"**-GirlGirl-**: No way!!"

Her chat screen continued to flood with comments from fans. These ranged from cheers for this latest twist in the theater of war to the sort of random abusive comments women gamers always faced. And, of course, spam.

"DerkWerk: You're a fraud!"

"Yalta187: Affirmative action at its finest."

"ManTan1997: Win a new phone, DM me to find out how!"

Bugz paid them no mind, her awareness completely consumed with setting a trap for the approaching horde. With a slight nod of her head, she conveyed to the Thunderbird the arcing flight path she wanted her to take. Closing her eyes, she marshaled every other living being in this virtual landscape to her side.

CHAPTER 2

"How does she do it?" Feng asked. Though he stood among his clan brothers, all of whom were blocked from pursuing Bugz for a moment by the landslide, he wasn't speaking to any of them in particular. Feng's virtual assistant assumed the question was directed at it and popped to life in his heads-up display, launching a user-generated video tutorial explaining the 'Verse.

"The Floraverse is different from other virtual worlds before it," the young voice said over a montage of idyllic scenes from the Spirit World. His phone played the English language video inside his visor and translated the audio instantly into Mandarin for his earbuds. Feng scanned the battlefield and half ignored the feat of computer translation. "Rather than letting users build their environment out of minerals and tools, or forts and wood, the game engine that powers the Floraverse is modeled after living, growing things . . ." Feng swiped past the video and on to another one as he began to climb the boulders the avalanche had left in his way. This video was labeled "The Bugz Conspiracy."

"While many other players in this world seek to exploit the Floraverse, Bugz lives in concert with it, appearing to be able to call anything she can imagine into existence," an on-screen host intoned. Feng's boot slipped momentarily from a crevice. He stumbled and regained his footing as the host continued. "No one knows exactly how she does it, but the result is that she has become the best player the game has ever known."

Feng, now running atop the rockslide, skipped ahead in the video playlist. After a two second pre-roll ad for a new phone, another video began, this one called "Bugz's Top 10 Creations." The narrator from the first video returned. "While other players struggle to build an arsenal that might include a few weapons and an animal to ride around on, Bugz, in her time in the Floraverse, has become the GOAT. She doesn't ride a donkey; she rides supernatural beasts. Rumor has it her Indigenous identity plays a big role—she taps into the collective consciousness of her Ancestors. Her greatest weapon is not a gun or knife but her ability to summon all the virtual beings around her and create things no other player can imagine."

"Hey, Bugz's #1 fan," a member of Clan:LESS named Joe said to Feng with a mocking smile. "Yeah, I saw you freeze up when you fell and she made eye contact with you." Joe batted his eyelashes. "I know you love her. But you run faster when you're not watching videos."

"Shut up," Feng responded with a laugh. He swiped the video window closed and ran harder. He felt good that a clanmate he looked up to had been watching him, even if it came with a little razzing. Feng put his head down and sprinted to catch up to his clanmates.

CHAPTER 3

Bugz's legendary status was only as good as her last battle, and this time she knew she faced a huge challenge. Confidence and talent could only go so far when you were this badly outnumbered. The angry pack of clanmates chasing her had started out wanting her riches, but now after her ambush they'd surely want revenge too. They wouldn't stop at simply defeating her either . . . they needed to humiliate her.

"Down there!" she said, pointing with her lips in traditional Anishinaabe fashion, to a lake that spread from the foot of the mountain and on to the horizon. The Thunderbird sped to within a few feet of the water's surface. The first soldiers of the Clan:LESS horde poured over the mountaintop. The reflection of the winged giant shone across the water as Bugz and the Thunderbird flew by. The moonlight and the starry sky above lit the surroundings magically, the atmosphere amplifying every movement of the combatants below.

Laser beams sped past and bullets pierced the waves. Bugz named her home base Lake of the Torches in part because of the way the stars and moons danced across the waters. It reminded Bugz of her father teaching her to torch fish as a girl. Now, with an unholy military apocalypse raining down, the lake's name took on a new meaning. The tracers of gunfire reflected back at the heavens as laser beams shone into the waters and scattered into oblivion.

The Thunderbird banked back toward the mountain as Bugz dove from her back and plunged deep beneath the waves.

"Get into the water!" Alpha yelled as the Clan:LESS horde reached the shores of the lake. Some pulled personal submersibles and scuba gear from their packs and plunged into the waters to pursue their target. Others assembled and launched gunships, tracking Bugz from the surface. On board one such ship, equipped with a massive cannon, Alpha set out to a spot where he guessed she might re-emerge. Flashlight and spotlight beams swept frantically across the surface of the lake as the search for Bugz continued—to no avail. Alpha and his crew saw nothing in the black waves except the reflections of the lights above. After five minutes, the excitement died down, and a deathly quiet settled on the water.

A rumbling began deep beneath the surface.

"She's coming up!" The radio channel connecting all of the members of Clan:LESS crackled to life with a dispatch from one of the submersibles.

"Everyone train your sights on the target," Alpha shouted across the waves. He located the radio signal flashing on his map and pointed to a spot on the lake. The rumbling grew louder.

"Give us an update," Alpha yelled into his mic, his voice betraying a hint of nerves.

Silence spread across the radio channel as the sound of the rumble only increased.

Suddenly, the lake roared. The water frothed and parted as a massive snake tore through the surface, shooting into the sky above. It roared like a giant lion. This fierce, scaled creature looped high into the air and traced a Ferris wheel path against the stars above. The Clan:LESS soldiers stared in frozen awe, and remained that way for several seconds as the creature continued to arc across the heavens.

The snake reached the pinnacle of his flight path and turned back toward the soldiers, slowly at first but soon with an increasing and terrifying speed. He screamed again. In this instant, the beast showed his face to the mercenaries below, his head that of a giant panther crowned with two menacing horns. To some of the soldiers, he must have resembled a saber-toothed devil; others recognized him from the rock paintings flashing on their screens during tutorial videos. Either way, the soldiers did not move.

"FIRE!" yelled Alpha, charging his energy cannon.

One by one, the members of Clan:LESS sprang into action. They fired into the sky, but it amounted to nothing. Before they could train their sights on the creature, he struck. The horned serpent plunged into one of the gunships and ran through the soldiers on board. Clan:LESS fighters were tossed from his path like grass from a lawn mower. He carried the remnants of the boat deep underwater. Dozens of gamertags flew toward the sky as members of Clan:LESS departed the Spirit World. Silence returned for a moment before the leviathan resurfaced underneath another boat and trapped it in his jaws, shaking it from side to side in the air like a dog playing with a stick.

This beast was Mishi-pizhiw, perhaps the most intimidating of Bugz's creations.

Mishi-pizhiw dove out over the water and his body crashed down across a huge tranche of the Clan:LESS armada. More than a hundred gamertags evaporated upward. In an instant, with the contours of the battle now shifted, Bugz was owning Clan:LESS.

"Retreat!" Alpha screamed, diving into the water just moments before the razor-sharp fins on Mishi-pizhiw's back tore his boat in half. The ensuing wake swamped Alpha's energy cannon. It blinked on and off listlessly a few times before sinking into the lake, never to be seen again. One of the remaining boats plucked Alpha from the waves as he and the surviving members of Clan:LESS made a break for the shore.

Once Alpha was safely on board the boat, Bugz heard him scream to his followers, "This is not a retreat, we are simply regrouping! We must always win!"

CHAPTER 4

Their horde now wrecked, Feng and the other Clan:LESS survivors beached their boats on the shore. He looked over his shoulder at the water-borne beast bearing down on them. Neither he nor any of his clanmates saw Bugz directly ahead of them, swinging her obsidian sword, until the first heads began to roll. More gamertags ascended to the heavens.

Feng tripped as he jumped off the boat and fired blindly behind him. From his hands and knees, he struggled onto the muddy shores of Lake of the Torches to reload his gun, cursing to himself as he went.

"Regroup on the far side of the mountain!" shouted one of Alpha's henchmen, carrying their injured boss across his shoulders like a firefighter. Feng touched the raised Ø branded onto his arm.

"Well, they say Alpha likes to get carried away." Joe

grinned at his own dad-joke as he ran by in the direction of the retreating soldiers.

As Feng tried to get back to his feet, he saw a pair of sleek black shoes before him. Emblazoned on their vamps—in the style of traditional Anishinaabe moccasins—was a design familiar to many across the Floraverse: a neon-pink flower adorned by Day-Glo-green leaves. He looked up past the shoes, and past their owner's hips, ripped torso, and shoulders.

"Bugz?" Feng asked, locking eyes with her. He sounded like a monk blessed by a visit from the Almighty. He shuddered as he exhaled.

"Don't get all kissy-faced on me now. You're making this awkward." Bugz's sword had already plunged through the top of Feng's virtual skull before she finished speaking.

"You have been eliminated by Bugz. You cannot respawn at this time."

The words flashed across Feng's display. He watched helplessly as Bugz ran off and dispatched another five of his clanmates at close range. In this moment Feng lost everything invested in his virtual life—years of his personal time and all of his money. But he felt neither rage nor frustration. He couldn't help but admire how perfectly Bugz leapt from technique to technique, effortlessly thinning the ranks of Clan:LESS soldiers.

CHAPTER 5

Bugz ran back up the steep mountain in pursuit of the escaping members of Clan:LESS. But now, the forest creatures ran at her side. Moose, elk, and bears trampled and mauled the Clan:LESS soldiers. Smaller animals teamed up to take down enemies in their own almost-cartoonish fashion. A particularly embarrassing replay would show one clanmate taken down by a pack of rabbits and squirrels. Even the roots and vines grew speedily up the hill and enveloped the slowest of the retreating warriors, trapping them and suffocating them, turning their 'Versonas into plant food. Mishi-pizhiw transformed into his land form, that of a giant panther with diamondback plates running down his spine. He joined the chase for a moment but soon turned back to the lake, the battle already decided.

Bugz was hunting the last fifty or so Clan:LESS soldiers when a spaceship landing on the far side of the summit captured her attention. Clan:LESS planned to evacuate. They wanted to live to fight another day.

"I guess the bot can handle it from here," she said to her online followers. She addressed her virtual assistant: "Shoot to kill, but don't pursue them into space. Guard Lake of the Torches until I return."

As the artificial intelligence system took over and gifts of gold and diamonds flooded her chat screen, Bugz pulled her VR headset off and shook her hair back to the way she liked it, with a side part framing one eye. She'd returned to the real world.

Bugz's bedroom doorway framed the figure of her brother, Waawaate, who stood there grinning.

"Hey, nerd. Come and eat." His invitation hung in the air as he turned to leave.

Bugz grabbed a half-empty bag of chips from her messy bedroom floor and chased him up the stairs to join her family for supper.

ONE YEAR
LATER

CHAPTER 6

"Alright, ladies and gentlemen." The pow-wow emcee's voice boomed over the massive sound system. "This young lady makes us all very proud with her talent online in what they call that vir-chew-al reality. And now, coming from a good pow-wow family, she wants to give back to the community in the Anishinaabe way. So she's gonna dance in her jingle dress one time through and then all the other junior women's jingle dress dancers are gonna join her for the last three push-ups of the song."

I'm having an anxiety attack, Bugz thought. She often felt this way outside the Floraverse. Bugz did her best to keep it together in her jingle dress—black with pink-and-green beadwork accented by her metal-cone jingles. She pictured the many elegant Anishinaabe women she'd seen before. She knew their look: dignified, beautiful, calm— just like her mom. While she tried to focus on projecting that image externally, the inside of her head rat-a-tat-tatted a loop of her greatest insecurities. She would soon dance in front of all these people, solo. *How many are there, a thousand?* She felt the stares of everyone around the pow-wow arbor. Were they focused on her belly rolls? Of course her mom had lied to her earlier when she said Bugz looked great in this regalia. *I look fat. I feel fat. I am fat.*

Oh great, now I'm starting to sweat. Bugz's internal monologue flared into full red-alert. She chastised herself for the need she felt to project an image of extreme poise. *Gotta make the grandmas proud, right?* But she could definitely feel sweat. Under her arms, running down her back. A hot, sweaty, sticky mess. *Great.*

"Ladies and gentlemen, it is our pow-wow way, when one of us receives a great gift, as this young lady certainly has, our culture calls on us to give back with a giveaway ceremony and by sponsoring a pow-wow special like this one. Of course, we all watched her grow up dancing in the jingle dress, the healing dress . . ."

Of course the emcee has to go on and on. They always do. Nothing a pow-wow emcee liked better than to expound on every single detail of their teachings, to thank every blade of grass with their prayers, and to even explain their corny jokes.

"Yes, ladies and gentlemen, it is the pow-wow way . . ."

Isn't the pow-wow way to dance and sing? Why all the talking? And why am I so negative right now? Gotta think positive. Well, at least I'm wearing black. No one can see I'm

26

a sweaty mess. Unless my makeup starts running. God! I wish I could check myself in my phone right now.

"So, at this time we are going to ask the Lodge Pole Singers to give us that jingle dress song . . ."

Boom!

The sound of the big drum echoed over the PA system, reverberated around the Rez, and rang out across the universe. The drummers picked up a fast beat and the lead singer belted out a crisp, clear lead that the half-dozen other singers around him grabbed and blasted back to him. Bugz recognized the song immediately—the original jingle dress song given in a dream to her people generations ago.

Bugz jumped to the balls of her feet and started to dance. Instantly, her nerves and anxieties dissipated, washed away by the swishing sounds of the dozens of metal cones fastened to her dress. The baseball-park lights surrounding the arbor flared in a million directions from the jingles as they swung and swayed with Bugz's every move. She hit a quick double-time pattern with her feet to accentuate the contours of the song's melody. With one hand on her waist and the other gripping a fan of spotted eagle feathers, she lost track of all her worries, focusing deeper, only on the moment she inhabited. No more self-doubt, no more crowd of onlookers . . . just her and the drum. For once, Bugz even stopped thinking about the Floraverse and her phone.

In her mind's eye, Bugz transformed into the visionary young woman who'd received the jingle dress so long ago. *The healing dance.* Bugz scanned the sidelines and saw the other dancers waiting to join in. Most of these young women danced on the contest pow-wow trail all summer long. Some of Bugz's cousins even made a living this way, making car payments and paying rent with their prize money. But as she took in the proud smiles in the Elders' seating section of the crowd, Bugz knew that here, in this part of Anishinaabe country, the jingle dress meant something deeper. Here, it was more than a dance . . . it was closer to a religion. The people here still believed the jingle dress dancers could make sick people well. The people here still offered tobacco to jingle dress dancers for their relatives who wanted to sober up. The people here still spoke of how this dance would heal their nation from the hangover of colonization. And so Bugz danced, for her family, her people, her way of life.

The honor beats struck, loud drum beats accentuating the rhythm of the song, and Bugz raised her eagle fan high in the air. She swung it from side to side with the downbeats as though brushing the pain and sickness from her community in one direction, *boom, boom, boom,* and then lifting their spirits back up in the other direction, *boom, boom.* As the honor beats ended, she kept her fan in the air for a moment. Her jingles splayed in all directions, the eagle plume in her hair danced in the breeze, and her expression froze with the realization of her inheritance. In this moment, Bugz found peace. She no longer projected the image of a strong Anishinaabe woman—she simply shone the light of her spirit on all those around her.

As the singers at the big drum started the next push-up, or cycle, of their song, two dozen other young jingle dress dancers stepped from the periphery and into the center of the arbor to dance their styles. Each used the same basic steps, but just as their regalia featured colors and designs that brought their personalities into stark relief, so too did their moves embody the uniqueness of their characters. Together, these women inspired an invisible wave of pride to sweep across the crowd. A round of applause broke out.

"Ladies and gentlemen, let them know if you like what you see . . ."

Of course the pow-wow emcee can't let a beautiful moment pass without trying to put his stamp on it. Bugz's internal monologue rebooted, but her pow-wow spirit overrode it. She was on autopilot and would dance to the end of the song in fine form. For five minutes, she defeated her anxiety.

Bugz glanced at the emcee stand on the east side of the arbor and glimpsed her parents. They stood in the same spot as twelve years earlier, when Bugz had walked out into the circle in ceremony, when her community welcomed her into the pow-wow circle for her first dance and followed her around the arbor for the first time. Her father, Frank Holiday, in jeans and a baseball cap, stood with his chest wide and smile wider. Her mother, Summer, stood to the right, wearing one of those cheesy smiles Bugz saw on parents recording videos of their child's first steps. Bugz studied her mother, the very picture of Anishinaabe royalty. Summer wore a Pendleton jacket, a white cowboy hat, and an eagle-whistle necklace adorned with beautiful beadwork.

Bugz eyed the whistle, made from the wing bone of a bald eagle, a ceremonial item sacred to those on the pow-wow trail and to the Anishinaabe way of life. Bugz longed for her mother to pass it on to her. Bugz wanted it so bad she licked her lips, triggering a hunger as old as she could remember. Perhaps in a few more years.

Bugz's mom looked like an Anishinaabe princess, but she meant more to her people than a simple figurehead. She led the community as an elected Chief. Every few minutes, some member of the crowd would walk up and shake her hand. Bugz, still dancing, spun in place and returned her gaze to her parents, remembering an old story she'd heard from when they first dated. At that time, her mom worried whether she should really take Frank's last name or whether it would sound too much like a joke.

"Chief Summer Holiday," Bugz whispered to herself. Good choice. Her mom lived up to the cool name.

The last check beats of the song rang out across the arbor as all twenty-five young women waved their fans in the air. The drum finished and the dancers ended in synchrony, like gymnasts sticking their landings—an army of Anishinaabe women healing the nation.

CHAPTER 7

Later that night, after Bugz finished handing out gifts and prizes from her pow-wow special, she bumped into a group of young women in fancy shawl regalia—shiny dresses in bright colors adorned with brighter, shinier beadwork. Each had hair pulled back tightly into unique braided patterns. Bugz scanned their makeup.

"Omigod, what a crazy special, Bugz." Stormy, the crew's leader, barely looked up from her phone as she spoke. "I've never seen anyone give away a car for a prize in a special."

"Well, they did once in New Town." This correction came courtesy of Stormy's best friend, Chalice, also speaking from behind a phone.

"But that's different. That was a raffle. Bugz gave a car for a dance contest! I wish I danced jingle!"

"Thanks." Bugz squirmed. "I guess . . . that's the cool

thing about the stuff I do online. I can do cool stuff in the real world too."

Bugz tried to figure out what they wanted. They never spoke to her at school, since they were a few years older. Bugz glanced at her phone and immediately back to the young women standing around her. *How are they all skinny? Do skinny girls hang out with each other exclusively?* Bugz's gaze lingered on their slender forms. The thought registered with her that they were the way Anishinaabe women should look. *At least that's what we look like in* Pocahontas *and the movies.* Bugz studied the earth in front of her, lost in thought. *You never see a chubby Cherokee princess in cartoons.*

"Wow, Bugz, you're so pretty in the 'Verse!" Stormy smiled.

Bugz looked up from her feet and saw a mirror image of her own 'Versona looking back at her from the clear seven-inch glass panel clutched in Stormy's hand. Stormy's eyes were softer now that she saw Bugz through the filter of her Floraverse skin. Bugz said a tiny prayer of thanks for the mediation of Stormy's phone. This window into the augmented reality they all inhabited through their 'Versonas served as a lifeline, connecting Bugz to a state in which she felt a little more relaxed.

Bugz raised her phone in kind, a similar-sized glass pane powered by the CPU hidden in the watch on her wrist. The looking glass sprung to life, displaying the filter of Stormy's 'Versona in front of the young woman and letting everything else behind it pass through uninter-rupted to Bugz's eye. *She's as beautiful in the real world as she is in the 'Verse*, Bugz thought. As Stormy pulled out a vape pen, looked to Chalice and then back to her feet, Bugz's phone showed her the augmented Stormy doing the same with perfect synchronization. Even when Bugz dropped her phone clumsily, wishing she could die in the process, the device accurately displayed Stormy's 'Versona to Bugz during the split second it fell, like a tumbling portal into a hidden world.

Bugz grabbed her phone and scanned the other girls quickly. They all wore 'Versonas purchased from a famous influencer and customized superficially. Through her phone, Bugz saw an Arianna with longer eyelashes, an Arianna with poutier lips, and an Arianna with a face tattoo. *Noobs*. No real gamer would be caught dead in an off-the-rack skin like these. A real gamer would have designed their own skin, like Bugz did.

Again, Stormy gave an approving, if absentminded, nod to Bugz's 'Versona. After spending years cursing her belly fat and studying her profile in the mirror, Bugz had poured a ridiculous number of resources into perfecting her 'Versona with a lean, trim waist. Stormy angled her phone down slightly to study Bugz's digital form before lowering her phone completely, revealing Bugz as she appeared in the real world. Bugz felt vulnerable. She wished she could return to the Spirit World, the higher plane of virtual reality in the Floraverse where she would be untethered from the real-life location to which she was currently bound in augmented reality.

"You can look at me through your phone if you want," Bugz said.

Stormy raised her phone again, a smile returning to her face, and pulled a long drag from the pen. She blew the vape smoke down toward her moccasins as she glanced knowingly at her friends and back to Bugz.

"So, how's your brother?" Stormy asked.

Oh, that's why she's talking to me, Bugz thought. *God, how perfect are her eyelashes? They look like the eyelashes of a camel in the desert, long enough to keep a sandstorm out.*

"Waawaate? He's alright," Bugz managed to spit out. She looked at the young women around her and made mental notes about how she might improve her skin. "Probably getting ready for his special. I think it's later tonight."

"We're definitely going to check that out. Your brother is *such* a good dancer." Stormy continued scrutinizing Bugz's appearance through her phone.

"Good looking, too," Chalice piped up.

"Gross." Bugz tried to stop the girls from going on any further.

One of the girls imitated the wolf-whistles heard in movies.

"Cut it out," Stormy cut in a little too loudly. "You know you're not supposed to whistle at night."

"Don't tell me you believe those stories." Chalice rolled her eyes for effect before rolling them back to her phone. She swiped her thumb, sending dozens of pictures, videos, and text messages flying by on her transparent screen.

"Well, they say if you whistle at the northern lights, they'll come and take you away," Bugz responded.

"Well, your brother's name means 'northern lights' . . . so maybe he'll come take *me* away." Chalice grinned and pretended to whistle again.

"Shush!" Stormy started fanning herself. "Don't mess around with that. Even if you don't believe, then at least don't whistle around the pow-wow at night. My kookom will come and yell at us!"

"Your grandma's scary," Bugz said.

"Junior Women's Fancy Shawl, you're up next." The pow-wow emcee's voice bellowed into the darkness of the outer ring of the pow-wow circle, where the young women stood.

"Well, I guess we got to go." Stormy blew another cloud of vape smoke into the air above where they stood. She flipped the view on her phone, turning it into a mirror. She checked her eyebrows and contour, hit the AR button in the corner, and watched her face become filtered through the Floraverse. "Perfection!"

"Tell Waawaate we said hi!" Chalice said through a smile that didn't reach her eyes.

"Omigod, Chalice! Don't be so basic!" Stormy shook her head at her friend. "Obviously she's going to mention this conversation to him."

The fancy shawl dancers laughed to one another as they made their way to the pow-wow arbor.

CHAPTER 8

"You've got some new friends?" Waawaate walked toward Bugz in his grass dance regalia, long fringes flowing like prairie grass from his shoulders, arms, and legs. Beads hanging from a headband ringed his eyes. A long porcupine-hair roach sat atop his braided hair. Bugz craned her neck to look up at her brother as he stood beside her. He'd inherited their dad's height and their mother's looks. Bugz wondered for a moment what she'd inherited, but quickly reminded herself she'd made out alright.

"You know those girls ain't trying to be my friend." Bugz laughed. "God, they are so in *looove* with you." She accentuated the long vowel by batting her eyelashes and mimicking a cartoonish look of adoration.

"Get outta here," Waawaate shot back with a smile.

"Omigod, you just love it, don't you?"

"Why not?"

"Because they're just using you to get to me and my money. That's why not." They both laughed. Bugz wished she could relax like this around other people. She raised her phone and studied the world around her. She called up her 'Versona and tweaked her eyelashes and hair to look more like Stormy's.

Waawaate interrupted her. "Let's go watch this drum group."

Bugz kept her phone in front of her as she followed her brother to the crowd of people who'd gathered to watch a group of singers. Waawaate stood next to a woman, a stranger to them. Bugz glanced at her briefly, noting her complexion, doe-eyes, and expensive but understated clothing. Bugz turned to the drum and whispered from the corner of her mouth to her brother.

"Who's that?"

"I think she's the new doctor. Just moved here," Waawaate said as he livestreamed the singers on his phone.

Their dad walked up to the crowd around the drum group just as the song finished. He nodded to Bugz and Waawaate.

"You guys want a ride home soon?"

"Sure," Bugz replied.

"I think I'm going to hang out for a bit after my special." Waawaate retied his head roach in preparation for his time to shine.

"Yeah, I think you better. Wouldn't want to disappoint your fans." Bugz grinned.

"Fans? You internet famous now too?" their father asked.

"*Fans*, dad." Bugz quickly gestured with her lips in the direction of the fancy shawl dancers clearing the arena. The young women failed to conceal their repeated glances at Waawaate.

"Oh." Her dad laughed. "Well, they do say we're supposed to dance for the people . . . and they are people, so . . ."

Bugz shot a look of embarrassment at her father. She noticed Waawaate rubbing his thigh.

"What's the matter?"

"My leg hurts. I hope I can get through the song."

"Probably tired from running through their heads all day." Bugz's father laughed at his own joke. Bugz rolled her eyes from behind her phone's screen.

"No, never mind. Should be fine," Waawaate grunted.

"Junior Men's Grass special, you're up next. Get ready." The emcee's voice rang out into the night.

"That's me." Waawaate walked out into the arbor.

The new doctor stepped in front of Bugz and her father.

"Hi, you must be Dr. Turukun." Bugz's dad extended a fist bump.

"Hi. I'm Liumei. How are you?"

"Pretty well, thanks for asking. I'm Frank Holiday, and this here is my daughter, Bugz. Pleased to meet you."

"Nice to meet you too. Bugz, you dance beautifully." Liumei's eyes scanned Bugz's jingle dress. "What do the designs on your costume represent?"

"Regalia, actually." Bugz corrected her as her dad winced almost imperceptibly. "Costumes are for clowns. We wear regalia."

"Right," Liumei said. "I'm used to people getting it wrong about my culture too. I'm super sorry. I shouldn't have said *costume*."

"It's fine."

Bugz's father jumped in. "So, how are you liking life on the Rez?"

"Well, your community's very beautiful. Everyone's super nice. The family I stayed with for the first few weeks took me fishing." Liumei glanced around. "And to be quite honest, it's not what I was expecting. It's not like any Rez I've seen on the news."

"My wife is doing an amazing job of creating work in our community. And our people have always been proud of our culture. So we're doing good."

A group of flies swarmed the lights above them, seeming to accent the awkward pause in the conversation.

"This your first time at a pow-wow?" Bugz's dad asked.

"No, I went to some at university," Liumei answered, a little too quickly.

Bugz could tell Liumei was lying. *Why do adults tell lies like this so often?* A smart, independent woman— someone who would be treated no differently even if she admitted she hadn't seen a pow-wow before—still felt compelled to tell a little white lie. *Bizarre.*

"Cool. Do you like grass?"

40

"What?" Liumei paused, looking confused.

"Grass . . . men's grass. My son's going to dance right away."

"He's really good," Bugz jumped in with a smile. She decided she liked Liumei because of her attempts to fit in and not in spite of them.

"Make sure you pay attention to his moves. He'll mirror everything he does on the left side on the right side a few beats later." Bugz's father stared into the centre of the dance arbor as he spoke. "It represents keeping everything in balance in the universe."

CHAPTER 9

"So, at this time, the pride of our Rez, Waawaate Holiday, is going to put on a demonstration for all of you, and then we'll get into his special. And, ladies and gentlemen, he has requested a trick song, so let's see who wins this showdown—the dancer or the drummers. Okay, we've got the high sign."

With that announcement from the emcee, the next drum group picked up a new song, this one faster than the one Bugz had danced to, and Waawaate kicked his legs out from underneath himself, spinning to his left and causing the long fringes on his regalia to whirl around. The drummers hit a loud honor beat and Waawaate stopped on a dime, paused for the fringes to complete their swing and immediately spun in the opposite direction. The crowd roared its approval. Bugz glanced over at the fancy shawl dancers and saw they all had their phones out. They were livestreaming her brother. *I wonder how many followers they have?*

As the honor beats struck, Waawaate worked himself lower to the ground, almost doing the splits as he rolled his shoulders in time with the rhythm. Halfway through the downbeats he popped up, spun around, and, this time facing the opposite direction, worked himself low again.

Bugz looked to her father and noticed a twinkle in his eyes.

"Hey, Dad, you crying?"

Frank paused for a second.

"Guess I am . . ."

Bugz loved her dad's honesty. She knew her father had played an alpha male role in his youth: all-star athlete, valedictorian, and, according to some rumors Bugz heard, maybe a little rough around the edges at times. But now she saw a middle-aged man playing a supporting role to his wife's leadership ambitions, and apparently in touch with his emotions too.

"I guess it's just nice to see someone you raised up from a baby learn this way of life. And do it so well."

Waawaate strode in place, running-man style. Spectators sprinted from the bleachers and laid twenty- and fifty-dollar bills at his feet. In response, he kicked the money away with his moccasins and the crowd roared even louder. Even more people ran out to lay money down.

"Watching you kids dance makes me feel like our culture is going to survive another generation." Frank paused to soak up the sight of his son killing it on the dance floor. "Those are still my moves, though."

Bugz admired her dad's efforts to bring the conversation back to a lighthearted note. Still, she couldn't resist.

"Dad," she said with a huge grin on her face, "you could never dance that good."

Bugz felt her dad pulling her closer to him. As the drum group cut off its beat unexpectedly, Waawaate ended his dance in perfect time to the trick stop of the music. To call attention to his mastery of the song, he struck a pose, both arms pointing to the left, like a professional wrestler vamping for the crowd.

"Hiii chaaa!!!" Waawaate yelled to the sky.

The crowd roared louder than they had all evening.

CHAPTER 10

Feng fell hard on the mat of the virtual dojo, brought down by a hulking behemoth with twin Ø tattoos on his biceps. The Behemoth followed Feng to the mat after his double-leg takedown, trapping Feng's legs in the process. Feng rolled to his side and pushed, furiously attempting to escape by sliding his hips away from his opponent. A wasted effort. The Behemoth, still gripping Feng's legs, slipped forward like a base runner sliding into home plate. A quick spin later and he straddled Feng, sinking in a choke. From here, it seemed like a formality. Feng tapped out a few seconds later to avoid the complete strangulation of his 'Versona.

They fought in the Clan:LESS training center, a mixed martial arts gym housed in an airplane hangar on the clan's Floraverse compound. They trained alongside countless clanmates for the rematch with Bugz they planned to launch soon.

Feng and the Behemoth reset their starting positions on the mat and fist-bumped each other. This time, Feng anticipated his opponent's charge and sprawled out over top of him. He pushed the Behemoth's head down into the mat as the giant lunged forward. Feng spun and took the Behemoth's back and locked in a choke of his own. The giant struggled against Feng's grip.

"C'mon, just tap," Feng whispered. "Tap or nap."

The giant rolled once, twice, and three times, struggling to escape, but succeeded only in locking himself in the choke further. Finally, he tapped, and Feng quickly released his neck.

"Alright, good job, boys. Come circle up for a minute." Alpha's voice thundered across the training space. He sat down on the mat as the other Clan:LESS soldiers formed concentric circles around him, their 'Versonas sweaty from virtual training. "Let's review this battle plan again. Last time, we made the mistake of launching all our forces at her at one time. We saw she can throw countless resources at us if we crowd in one spot. This time, we'll space out our attack and make her fight on two fronts at once. She won't manage to keep up with both." Alpha spelled out the details of his new plan of attack, littering his speech with profanities and sexist language. That sort of talk always made Feng cringe but he never said anything about it in the hopes it would help him fit in.

After the strategy session ended, Feng sat at the edge of the mat relaxing with a couple of fellow clanmates.

"You guys ever move far from home?" Feng asked.

"Nah. What you mean?" the Behemoth grunted.

"I'm leaving China."

"Really?" Feng's friend Joe asked.

"Yeah," Feng replied. "I'm on the plane right now. In-flight Wi-Fi is kind of bunk. That's the only reason you got a round on me, Behemoth."

"Yeah, right." His training partner chuckled.

"Where you moving to?" Joe asked.

"Your mom's." The Behemoth giggled.

"Shut up." Joe threw a boxing glove at the offending clanmate. "So what happened, Feng? Seemed like you were such a stan for China, always talking about the evils of 'the West.'" Joe air-quoted the last two words for full emphasis.

"Oh, I still think you guys are lazy." Feng laughed. "And I still love China." Feng bit his lip. "Just maybe not the party that runs it." He scratched the back of his neck.

"What happened?" asked Joe.

Feng swallowed. He leaned closer to the pair huddled beside him. "Alright, but you guys can't tell anyone. Promise?"

Joe and the Behemoth nodded quickly.

"So . . . ," Feng began, scanning the room as though he might yet decide not to spill his guts, "I left because my family thinks I'll be disappeared."

"What do you mean 'disappeared'?" asked the Behemoth.

"Bro!" exclaimed Joe. "I saw this in a forum. It means abducted by the government. Like kidnapped. That right, Feng?"

Feng nodded.

"What for?"

"For being part of Clan:LESS, I guess."

"No way." Joe's face matched that of a child opening the world's greatest Christmas present. "Abducted by the government for being part of Clan:LESS. That's so awesome!"

Feng looked around the dojo, worried Joe's excitement would attract eavesdroppers. "Relax, buddy. It's not cool at all."

"So what happened?" Joe asked breathlessly.

"I got a visit from neighborhood officials with the party." Feng scanned his friends and judged their reactions as underwhelming. "They made me sign this." He opened a screenshot in midair, showing a statement with his signature visible at the bottom. "It says I won't do a bunch of things, including visit the Floraverse anymore, and it lists all my failings."

"Must be a long list." The Behemoth giggled. "Let me see." He screenshotted the document and pinch-zoomed to view it closely. "A long list of failings for real: subversive activities, terrorist sympathizer, terrible at grappling . . ."

"What?" Feng asked, surprised.

" . . . still sleeps with the nightlight on . . ."

"Shut up."

"So you left China for us," Joe exclaimed. "You're a soldier for real."

"Didn't have much choice. Next step would've meant waking up in a strange room handcuffed to a bed and forced to learn songs praising the party . . ." Feng sighed. "Uncle didn't want that, so next thing you know I'm on a plane to Turkey, changed planes there and now I'm on one headed across the Atlantic."

"Well, you know what Alpha always says—N.C.B.U.— nothing comes between us," the Behemoth said. "And 'bros first.' So, let us know if you need any help."

"No doubt," Joe added.

"I also don't have any doubts." Feng's automatic translator had a rare trip-up on this phrase. Of course, it escaped Feng's notice, because his phone presented the entire conversation to him in his native Mandarin. But the translator snapped back to fluid North American slang for his clanmates before Feng spoke again. "Clan:LESS for life. You guys always had my back. Even when no one else did, not even my parents."

"That's right, man. Brothers for life," the Behemoth said as they all fist-bumped. "Now let's go again." He rolled onto his back like a dog waiting for a belly rub.

Feng stood and cartwheeled over his outstretched legs. They were off sparring again.

CHAPTER 11

Bugz and Waawaate were sprawled out on a couch in their parents' living room. They shared the warmth of a Pendleton blanket as they scrolled through their phones, TV droning on in the background, neglected. Their house, though bigger than most, shared the same linoleum flooring as most others on the Rez. It smelled of cedar and home cooking. Braised meat, in particular.

Bugz's dad shouted from the kitchen, where he examined a moose roast bathing in a slow cooker. "You guys get off those things. Supper's almost ready."

Bugz and Waawaate exchanged glances, silently agreeing to ignore their father. After scrolling for another five minutes, their mother appeared in the living room.

"C'mon, kids, don't be like that. Your dad said supper's ready." Their mom did her best to look serious.

"*You* don't be like *that!*" Waawaate mocked in a

high-pitched voice, waving his finger with exaggeration to provoke his mother. Bugz giggled.

Their mom cracked a smile. "Seriously, though, let's eat."

"Can we just bring it in here?" Waawaate stood stiffly. Bugz noticed him stutter-step as though he'd stubbed his toe. She thought of his hip and the pow-wow.

"No, your dad worked hard on this dinner. He got the animal himself, but we're going to eat it together," their mom responded.

"Correction," Waawaate smiled. "The animal gave himself to us. That's what the Elders say. All Dad did was show up in the right place at the right time."

Their dad laughed genuinely. "Come in the bush with me next time and we'll see how easy you say it is after that."

"Must be. You did it." Waawaate grinned back at his father and threw his arm around his shoulder.

"Get the bowls, Survivor Man," their dad responded.

Bugz, with bowls already in hand, stepped closer to her father and brother. She basked in the family love as her dad ladled out the stew. Steam rose and clouded the glass surface of the phone she'd pulled from her pocket.

"Jeez, Buggy, can you put that thing away for two seconds?" her mother asked from the kitchen table.

"Sorry, Mom." Bugz slid the device into her pocket and placed a bowl on the table, nudging it toward her mother. She placed the second in front of herself and sat.

"Anama'edaa," her father said.

Bugz's mom said a quick prayer in Ojibwe, thanking the Spirits, Mother Earth, and the Creator for the meal—and, yes, the animal for giving his life to sustain theirs. As she finished, the family tore into their dinner.

"How's it going with the new school, babe?" Bugz's father asked her mother.

"Not bad, but we're hitting a snag with the government. They want us to do another needs assessment." Bugz chewed the tender meat and savored it as she listened to her mother speak. She loved moose, the finest of all wild meats as far as she knew. Her mother continued. "It doesn't make sense. Practically all the kids live on the Rez, and yet Bugz and Waawaate have to take the bus to the school in town."

"Same old story," Frank grunted. "It's not like they teach Anishinaabe kids what they need to know in school anyway."

"Well, that's the goal. Have a school that works for *us*."

"I don't know why we have to go to school anyways," Waawaate piped up. "We do most of our homework online."

"Correction," Frank said between bites. "You're *supposed* to do most of your school work online. Last I checked, you hadn't done anything." Everyone at the table smiled at the joke.

"I did *some*." Waawaate drew out his answer for laughs.

"Waawaate's right, though," Bugz said after she stopped giggling. "The only thing we really do together is first period, homeroom. The rest of the time we're just on our own, submitting assignments online and watching tutorials on our phones."

"It didn't used to be like that, you know." Frank rose and cleaned his bowl. "When your mom and I were kids, we were in big classes all the time with all the other students. All day. Every day. Then when we were in twelfth grade, bam, they canceled our school year. Can you imagine that? We never had a graduation."

"We had a grad," Summer said.

"Yeah, a virtual grad. But you know what I mean. We didn't get to go party with our friends, or walk across a real stage," Frank responded. "Anyways, that first pandemic changed things. The next two after that even more so."

"Thanks for the history lesson, Dad." Waawaate grinned. "And everything cost less than a dollar too, right?"

"School is basically just a warehouse for kids," Bugz said. "There aren't enough teachers to actually teach us. They're just trying to keep us off the streets and out of our houses so our parents can work."

"There's more to school than that," Summer spoke up, suddenly serious. "There's the social side too. You kids don't get away from your phones enough or out in the community. The school's good for that, at least. You go to town, you meet some of the kids who live there. You see something different."

"The difference is the kids from town all go home after homeroom and do their work from there, but us Rez kids, who don't live within walking distance, have to stick around the library or the hallways to do ours," Bugz said.

"There's things you share in common with those kids too." Frank smiled, thinking he'd spawned a PSA-worthy moment.

"Yeah, we're all bored and stare at our phones for fourteen hours a day," Waawaate griped good-naturedly.

"Waawaate," Summer said sternly.

"Sorry." Waawaate sat up straight. "Fourteen hours a day, except for Tuesdays and Thursdays when I have basketball. It's thirteen hours on those days."

Bugz couldn't help but laugh. Her older brother had always been her favorite form of entertainment.

After dinner, she dragged her school bag to the front door, stepped outside, and dove into the Floraverse.

CHAPTER 12

Bugz sat in the center of a ring of stones, a spot not far from her home on the Rez, though to anyone else it could've seemed like another planet and another time. This sacred space occupied a clearing hidden in dense woods. The lichen and moss testified to the generations over which these stones had sat in this place. The rocks varied in size, but the ones forming the core of the ring were bigger than large suitcases. Smaller rocks piled around them softened the edges of the petroform.

Bugz imagined her Ancestors who'd built this monument. When she was a child, her parents taught her to put tobacco down before a thunderstorm to give thanks to the Thunderbirds. Later, they brought her to this Thunderbird's Nest to pay homage to the thunder-beings protecting their homelands.

Bugz peered off into the tree line circling the edge

of the clearing. Her fingers gently tapped the moss around her, her eyes completely engrossed with the images her headset put before them. The device held her phone to her eyes like a VR helmet, but it also scanned her brain, translating her real-world thoughts into action inside the Spirit World of the Floraverse.

At the moment, her 'Versona was swimming deep in Lake of the Torches. As she thought about picking up speed, her avatar kicked powerfully in the virtual depths of the moonlit water. As she thought of a mermaid, her 'Versona pressed her legs together and thrust herself forward like a dolphin, adding speed again. Most players could only power simple moves like walking or running through their neural links, but Bugz, ever the virtuoso, knew how to shorten the distance between thinking and acting—at least in the Floraverse.

As her virtual self descended farther into the dark reaches of the lake, she could see it take shape—a giant simulated stone circle similar to the Thunderbird's Nest on which she sat in the real world. But the 'Verse's ring of fallen obelisks housed a different supernatural creature. As Bugz expelled a flurry of bubbles that floated toward the surface of the lake, an enormous pair of red eyes blinked to life. The scaly mouth beneath them broke into a grin. Suddenly, Mishi-pizhiw's dark form darted backward like a crayfish and swam around in a circle before meeting her.

"Hello, beautiful," Bugz said. She gripped the back of Mishi-pizhiw's horns and held on as he pulled her toward the petroform. Letting go, Bugz drifted smoothly toward the center of the virtual stone circle. Her eyes rolled back in her head as she entered a trance. The state intensified the closer she moved to the center. Soon, settling into the lake bed, electricity coursed through her body and behind her glazed eyes.

The lake bed in the center of the stone ring undulated and disappeared suddenly, leaving in its place a nexus to the real world. If Bugz hadn't been alone, an observer in the Floraverse could've seen her sitting in the center of Mishi-pizhiw's nest, her real-world self and the Thunderbird's Nest mirrored beneath her in the portal. The two worlds, now connected, revealed two sides of the same coin. Bugz felt tremendous power. Not power as she imagined presidents or rich people felt, but power like she felt in the Sundance ceremony—something bigger than any one person.

Bugz shook her head, amazed again that an ancient Anishinaabe spiritual site shared a counterpart in the virtual world of artificial intelligence and blockchain. She remembered her first time here, and how she'd discovered she could respawn her virtual self directly into the Spirit World, bypassing the grind of having to earn her way back from AR mode.

Bugz picked up a handful of clay from the lake floor. She blew on it, causing water to whip up the tiny virtual sand particles. This miniature whirlpool spun quickly and became a hatchet, an ax, and finally a giant tomahawk.

Bugz inspected the weapon and lowered her head. Suddenly, a bolt of lightning crashed from the sky and through the depths of the lake. It struck the tomahawk, leaving it glowing silver-blue with a newly imbued energy.

"Just like Thor," Bugz whispered to herself. She double-checked that her video and audio feeds were off. She always disabled her livestream when she came here. It was important to keep this secret. If others found her path to success in the Floraverse, Bugz knew they'd try to copy it—and water down the power of this place in the process.

Bugz tossed the tomahawk to the lake floor and made another. Years earlier, she'd created Mishi-pizhiw and many of her other allies the same way. Manufacturing weapons didn't make her heart sing the same way it did when she breathed life into those creatures—that work brought the Anishinaabe worldview back from the dead, after all—but it did pay the bills. After an hour, she gathered a few dozen of the giant axes in a net and swam back to the surface.

CHAPTER 13

A sleek black SUV kicked up a cloud of red dust down an old dirt road, its ocher tones made deeper by the warm sunlight of the beautiful summer day. A thin brick-colored film gathered across the vehicle's surface.

The air conditioner hummed gently as Feng rode with his aunt in silence. The colorful scenery blew by outside, muted by tinted windows. Farmers' fields, still green, gave way to more indigenous terrain: bush, creeks, swamps. After a two-hour-plus drive from the airport, they neared the Rez. Feng furrowed his brow at his phone.

"You know you're kind of like the Fresh Prince of Bel-Air." Liumei cracked a smile as she interrupted the silence.

"What?" Feng remained focused on the pane of glass in his hand.

"Well, he got in some trouble and his fam got scared and sent him to live with his auntie in a town called Bel-Air . . ."

Feng betrayed absolutely no hint of recognition. He suspected his automatic translator was lagging again. He felt annoyed his aunt spoke to him in English.

"That's the theme song to a show. Will Smith rapped it."

Nothing.

"Will Smith? Heard of him?"

"The president? Yeah, I heard of him." Feng finally looked up from the screen. "I thought people only knew him from memes."

His aunt laughed.

Feng chuckled and held his phone up to the moonroof. He stared at the "user location not found" error message on the screen and scrunched his forehead up in bewilderment. "Where are you taking me?"

"I told you. The Rez is called Biiwaabik," his aunt said. "It means 'metal' in the local language, because of the iron in the soil. Pretty smart, don't you think?"

Feng nodded through a forced smile and swiped at his glowing phone.

"Hey, put that thing down and talk to me for a bit."

"Okay." Feng tapped his leg on the floor of the vehicle.

"I know it's a pretty big change for you to come here . . ."

Feng's face settled into a faint scowl.

"But I told Uncle I'd take care of you. And besides, I think you'll like it here. The land is beautiful, and . . ."— Feng could see his aunt searching for a way to land the second half of her sentence diplomatically—". . . it'll give you a chance to think things over."

"What did you hear?"

"Just that there was some . . . trouble."

"Trouble?" Feng felt a fire kindle inside. He stared at his aunt. She bit her bottom lip and stared straight ahead. Feng knew she wanted to avoid his gaze, but he didn't look away. The SUV rolled on for a few hundred yards before she continued. "You said some hurtful things about our people."

Feng looked to the road ahead. "Not my fault some people can't let go of the past."

"Does that mean your mom and dad too?"

The fire flared up. "At least I got to go to school . . . outside of a mosque, I mean."

"I'm sorry, Feng." Liumei shook her head. Feng could see she was weighing different responses. Finally, she spoke. "You weren't taken to a school—that was a re-education center. They brainwashed you."

"I would've been brainwashed either way." Feng scowled back down at his phone and swiped. His face softened.

"Remember this?" Feng held up his phone up to reveal a photo of Liumei, more than a decade younger, tears streaked across her face. The poor quality of the photo testified to its age, and that it had been taken from a distance.

"Where's that from?"

"Remember when you were staying with us? One night you came running back to my parents' apartment." Feng tilted the phone back to examine the image. "I heard you slam the door. Then—bam, bam, bam—a loud banging on the other side of it." He pinch-zoomed the

picture slowly. "I snuck out of bed and took this photo."
He angled the screen back to Liumei.

His aunt's face turned serious. She focused on the
road in front of her. "I begged the authorities not to take
me." She shook her head slowly. "Your parents promised
to report me if I engaged in any more 'subversive activities.'" She appeared to stare at something far down the
road. "I left China the next week."

"That's when the trouble started for my parents."
Feng put a quiet punctuation mark on the end of the
exchange. He felt his aunt looking at him as he stared out
the window, the tires still humming beneath them.

"I remember your name was Aaliyah when I was
growing up," Feng said, turning back to her. "I remember
you changed it to Liumei when you were still living with
us in Xinjiang."

His aunt nodded. "I thought I needed to fit in."

"Maybe you were right," Feng said softly.

"No, it wasn't healthy. Pretending to be someone else."

"You haven't changed your name back."

"I'm proud of who I am—of who we are." Feng
noticed a faint hint of desperation audible in his aunt's
voice as she corrected herself. "But once I started school
under this name, and got my medical degree, and started
to practice . . . it's too hard to change it back now." Feng
studied her from the corner of his eye.

"Everyone here has a reason. Or an excuse. A story.
I hope you haven't become like them." Feng wondered

whether he'd just crossed the line with his aunt. He debated apologizing but he said nothing further.

"I'm not some outsider who doesn't care about Xinjiang. That will always be my home." Liumei slowed the cadence of her speech. "Even if I never go back." She appeared to contemplate this.

"Sorry." Feng examined his sneakers. "I didn't mean anything by it."

They flew over a deep pothole, and Feng felt his stomach drop. A few feet later the vehicle made a loud thump and found level ground again.

Feng watched his aunt check the rearview, and he glanced out his side mirror. He could see only a cloud of red dust behind them. His aunt spoke again. "Our family always planned to leave Xinjiang. We probably should've done it sooner, for your sake. But you're here now."

"Uncle should've let me go to Beijing."

"Feng, I don't think you understand how much things changed for us. In my lifetime, we were free, we practiced our faith, we spoke our language. Now we all speak Mandarin."

"What's wrong with Mandarin?"

"Nothing, but we have our own language."

"Well, we can all speak English now too." Feng waved his phone, calling attention to its ability to translate the conversation in real time. "So what?"

"It's just not right," Liumei said. "The party controls everything you do, where you go, when you can leave the house."

Feng sighed. "No argument there, believe me." He turned to look out the window at the countryside. "But why not let me live closer to where the action is, in Beijing, instead of here in the middle of nowhere?"

His aunt ran her hands through her hair. "Anyway, I didn't mean for this ride to get so intense." She took a deep breath. "My brother—your uncle—and I just want you to see there's more to life than . . . whatever you're up to online."

Feng thought of his clanmates. As the red earth and trees flew by, neither he nor his aunt spoke.

Feng stared through his phone to a spot just to their south. The screen lit up and bathed his face in a copper glow. The window his phone offered into the Floraverse showed a fountain of energy shooting up into the sky from a place just beyond the trees. It was an extraordinary sight, like nothing he'd seen before in AR.

"Whoa," Feng whispered. He tried to make sense of the power source spewing light into the sky behind the forest. Though he hadn't been aware of it a moment ago, it now consumed Feng's thoughts.

CHAPTER 14

"Infinity axes are a quarter bitcoin," Bugz said, referring to the last of the tomahawks she planned to sell. She stood atop a beautiful red mesa with a seven-foot-tall Amazon facing her.

"Of course, and can I get a selfie too, please?" the Amazon asked.

"Sure, no problem." Bugz leaned in for the screenshot.

"I watch your streams every day," the fan said, posing at her preferred angle. "When I'm in the 'Verse, I've always got the stream window open, and if I'm out there," she continued, referring to the real world, "I watch you on my phone."

"Cool." Bugz smiled. "I like your beadwork," she added, referring to the pink, blue, and red geometric patterns her fan wore on her cape and leggings.

"Thanks, they're Quechuan designs, from my Ancestors.

I want to be as fierce a warrior as you someday. You're such an inspiration."

"Good luck," Bugz said. She always tried to shower her fans with good vibes and to answer all their questions. It seemed like the right thing to do, and it was good for business. "Well, next time we're online together, put your name in the chat screen and I'll shout you out during the stream."

"Oh, okay, awesome! And thanks again." The fan picked up her giant tomahawk and flew off into the sky using a jetpack.

Bugz scanned the desert plain. She came here, far from Lake of the Torches, to conduct these sorts of transactions. She swiped her hands apart quickly to open a livestream.

"Hey, hope everyone's having an awesome day in the 'Verse. Just a quick update to say I'm all sold out, but I'm back again next week, same location. And a quick shout-out to everyone who came by today to hang out, buy something, or just take a look around. Big shouts to all of you—especially Big_L_N, SchroederCat, and PeruvianGoddess—for the pics. Tag me. Hit the Subscribe button. We'll see you soon."

Bugz closed the chat window and stared off into the distance. The mesa on which she stood was the only high ground for miles. In the west, a burning red sun began to set. It set untold millions of fine dust particles on the horizon ablaze. The virtual scene stirred Bugz's heart. She liked to come here to escape the challenges of the real world. Her first time climbing the mesa came after a run-in with a girl at school who lived in a town close to the Rez.

Now, standing again on the mesa in the 'Verse, Bugz opened a video recording of the interaction from her saved files. The security camera footage she'd hacked from the school showed two teenagers walking together. Bugz remembered how she'd looked up to the girl. *The popular one.* As the video approached the moment when her now former friend body shamed her, Bugz snapped the video window closed and looked back to the sunset. *Why the heck did I rewatch that?* she asked herself.

Darkness swallowed the light of dusk. The night sky looked so much more vivid in the 'Verse. Here, the Milky Way seemed to pulse with activity. Ringed planets appeared as though within reach. Shooting stars illuminated the land every few minutes.

The wind picked up and howled in the distance. Bugz tried to focus on the beauty around her, but found her thoughts dragging her back to the girl from the security camera footage. Bugz suspected there was some flaw at the core of her being. If only she could locate it and remove it, she could heal herself, like a surgeon.

The anxiety loop roared to life inside her head again. Bugz wondered why she kept dwelling on negative thoughts like these. *Does everyone do this?* Perhaps she simply couldn't get along with other young women. *No, that's not true.* She'd just spent the weekend before hanging out with her cousin Ally. Her beautiful cousin Ally. Bugz thought of the cut marks she'd noticed on her cousin's arms. Ally had rolled her sleeves down as soon as Bugz asked about the scars on her biceps, changing the subject. But Bugz knew what they meant. She'd heard kids at school talking about 'cutters.' For a moment, Bugz imagined plunging a knife into her own arm. She shook her head violently, shuddering at the thought.

Bugz took a deep breath. She'd always assumed people who felt the way she felt at that moment could trace it back to some sort of deep childhood trauma. Yet there was nothing in her own life that she could point to. Sure, life on the Rez wasn't glamorous. In fact, the gravel roads, mixed-breed dogs, and homes with cheap siding often looked like poverty to outsiders. But she'd grown up in a loving home wrapped with all the supports of a vibrant community and culture. She figured she had no right to feel like this.

The Floraverse sky lit up as a meteor dragged its green-and-yellow tail toward Lake of the Torches. Bugz sighed, her heart as heavy as a million pounds.

CHAPTER 15

"What do you see, Feng?" his aunt asked. She slowed the SUV to a crawl as they entered the main town site on the Rez. "Are you logged into the Floraverse?"

"God, Liumei, you sound like an old person." Feng scrunched his forehead at the pulsating energy radiating across the sky on his phone. "Yes, it is the Floraverse, AR mode."

"What do you mean?"

"Well, look." Feng angled his phone toward his aunt, energy still shooting up from behind the trees like a volcano. "AR is a layer on top of the real world. Augmented Reality." As he turned his phone back and forth in front of Liumei it revealed different parts of the hidden landscape all around her. "Now look at this," Feng said, swiping to another window to reveal his 'Versona, hard at work at Clan:LESS HQ. "This is the Spirit World. It's not tied to any real-world locations. Total Virtual Reality. VR. Only real gamers get into this one."

"So which one is the Floraverse?"

"Both. You start in AR and then progress to the Spirit World, but they're both within the Floraverse. You take your skin and money and experience points from AR into the Spirit World." Feng opened a chat window on his phone. He began typing a message to the other members of Clan:LESS but soon thought better of it, given what Liumei had just said about getting into trouble online. His clanmates were hardcore. His aunt wouldn't understand.

"So which came first?"

"The AR came first." Feng shifted. Suddenly his face lit up and he spoke more quickly. "To be honest, I don't know how adults can stand life without an AR layer on top. It's so boring without it."

"You sound like an addict."

Feng betrayed no hint that he knew what she meant. "What's the point of the game?" she asked.

Feng paused. "What's the point of life?"

At this his aunt smirked. "To live to the fullest. To celebrate and work and meet wonderful people and love and laugh."

Feng blinked slowly at Liumei before resuming his rapid speech. "Anyway, the AR world is like a filter to make yourself look better, or whatever, and make the world around you more fun. But VR is where the missions and clans and a never-ending universe of possibilities takes place."

Feng tried to stop there, to remain silent, but he couldn't. His passion for the subject overtook him. "The 'Verse started as open-source. Hackers built it ages ago after the governments took over social media. Way back, during the pandemics."

"Hey! That wasn't that long ago. The pandemics are the reason I studied medicine."

Feng sighed. "Anyways, after all that *super*-ancient history"—he paused to let his gentle insult land—"hackers built an AR platform that no one could take over."

"Everything got so fragmented back then." Feng's aunt shook her head. "I can see why they wanted a new platform. Pretty smart."

Feng shrugged. "What's smart is they distributed it all across a blockchain. No central servers, no central authority." He grinned. "In the Floraverse, reality is a blockchain."

"'Reality is a blockchain.' Sounds deep. And why are you so pumped about that?"

"It means everyone who uses it has a piece of the Floraverse on our devices. We all constantly validate the presence of others through our own presence. Basically, we all create our reality together." Feng's face took on the smug look of a student completely schooling his teacher. His aunt didn't seem to mind.

Silence again, though this was more comfortable than the one they'd ridden through earlier.

"So is this why the neighborhood committee came after you? I can't imagine the party is too thrilled that you're consorting with a bunch of Westerners on an encrypted platform they can't monitor."

"Sort of."

"I bet." Feng could feel his aunt studying him. She spoke again. "How about this clan you're in? You met them in the VR Spirit World?"

"Stop calling it that. Again, you sound ancient. It's just the Spirit World." Feng actually sank into his seat at the sound of his aunt's un-coolness. "But yeah, I met them there. It's a big deal. They're famous—really good gamers." Feng deliberately tried to cast his clanmates in the best possible light. "You have to work your way up to the Spirit World, right? When you first start, it takes forever to get there. Someone destroyed me in the 'Verse about a year ago. After that, even as a good player, I only got back to the Spirit World a few weeks ago. It took so much work."

"I remember how frustrated I'd get when your mom would turn off my game and I'd lose my progress when I hadn't saved my Xbox for a few hours. So frustrating," his aunt added.

"Yeah, so imagine losing six months or a year's progress."

"Wow, I missed a lot while I was in med school and building a career. Here I thought AR was just for surgery assists, and you're telling me it's actually a path to the Spirit World. Nirvana!"

Feng couldn't help but smirk at his aunt's sarcasm. "Anyway, imagine all the graphics and data and history being blasted back and forth from user to user constantly chunked, processed, and added to the blockchain. It takes an awesome amount of computing power."

"Is that why you wear that clunky thing on your wrist?" His aunt smiled.

"Shut up. You wear one too, just like everyone else." Feng pointed to the smartwatch on her wrist for effect.

"But I don't use it to feel better about myself," she replied.

"That's a lie. Everyone uses their phone to feel better about themselves."

Feng's aunt steered the SUV into a gravel driveway. "Alright, here we are."

Feng got out of the car, stretched, and, following Liumei, dragged his roller-bag into the nondescript side-by-side the Rez provided to medical staff.

CHAPTER 16

The next day, Bugz watched a new student walk into her homeroom just before the morning bell. He sat at a desk next to hers, looking serious. She spotted some calligraphy sketched onto his binder with a Sharpie.

The newcomer turned to Bugz and introduced himself through his automatic translator: "Hello, I'm Feng."

"*Ni hao,*" she blurted out. Bugz felt embarrassed when Feng gave her a puzzled look. "Sorry. I don't know if you're speaking Mandarin. It's just something I learned online."

"No. It's cool. I'm just surprised. I didn't think anyone here would know any Mandarin . . . other than what the phone translates for you."

"What, the poor Indigenous folks wouldn't know anything about the wider world?" Bugz looked to the sky as she feigned a tone of indignation. "I am offended."

Feng smiled. "What's your name?" he asked, blushing as he spoke.

"Bagonegiizhigok Holiday." She forced a smile, feeling hot and self-conscious with the effort. *This guy's pretending not to recognize me from the 'Verse*, she thought. She could feel his gaze, like he was checking her out. *God, I hope I look okay.*

"So, you're new here?" Bugz cringed as the words left her mouth.

"Yeah, this is my first day." Feng stated what they both knew. His face turned serious, as though straining to think of a way to keep the conversation going.

"I—"

"D—"

They spoke simultaneously, cutting each other off. They both stopped after a syllable and apologized nervously.

"I'm sorry, you go."

"No, I wasn't going to say anything."

Bugz sighed and caressed her phone, a nervous habit. "So," Bugz began anew. "Where you staying in town?"

"Town? I moved to the Rez."

"Really?"

"What, a guy from China can't live on the Rez?"

Bugz giggled and looked down.

"Guess it's my turn to be offended." Feng smirked.

Bugz could feel Feng smiling at her and forced herself to look back up at him. As their gazes met, she felt like she looked more deeply into his eyes than she'd ever looked into anyone's eyes before—at least not without a screen in between them. She thought about the curved light reflecting back at her from his irises. For a moment, she felt so calm—her heart beat half a dozen times before her anxiety returned and the shyness enveloped her again.

"Guess we're both triggered then," she said, her cheeks turning red.

"Triggered," Feng repeated.

The teacher walked in and the class began. Feng turned to face the teacher, but for the rest of homeroom Bugz watched him from the corner of her eye.

CHAPTER 17

The moon shone high above Lake of the Torches, its reflection shimmering across rolling waves. Bugz paddled slowly in a birchbark canoe, pausing after each stroke to let the black water drip slowly back into the lake. The ripples from these droplets caught the dim light for a moment before they flattened into the nothingness of the expansive waters. Bugz and her canoe coasted smoothly through the simulated darkness of the Spirit World.

Overhead, the northern lights danced in the distance.

"Hello, Ancestors," Bugz whispered to them.

She blew air softly through her lips, increasing the pressure on her lower lip until she found a whistling tone. Bugz craned her head to the northern lights. She whistled the melody of an old prayer song she knew, one she learned from YouTube. She ran through it once and paused, gliding her canoe through the water, waiting for the virtual northern lights to respond to her tune.

Nothing.

"I guess they didn't program that into this universe," Bugz said to herself.

As her canoe drifted, a giant black diamondback surfaced in the water on her port side. Then another on her starboard side, and more behind her. As Bugz scanned the surface of the waters around her, dozens more shiny-plated beasts emerged from the dancing waters in every direction.

"Nameg." She whispered the Anishinaabe word for sturgeon. "You're so beautiful."

She paddled again.

"I love you all . . ."

Her voice trailed off as she scanned each of the prehistoric-looking life-forms around her, concentrating on paddling a weaving path between them.

"But which of you is my favorite?"

Suddenly, she noticed how quiet the Floraverse had become. She looked to the shore and saw a strange bounty hunter–looking 'Versona waving to her. *God, these fans,* Bugz thought. *Can't leave me alone.* The figure waved with greater urgency and brought their hands to their mouth, as though trying to yell. Bugz focused on what the person was saying. It sounded like "watch out."

She unmuted her chat.

Messages poured into her heads-up display.

"therealNix: Look out!"

"Feelthevern: They're about to attack!"

"Raven_womxn: Clan:LESS is closing in Bugz, pay attention!"

"Iamtheone: Stupid B—"

"Oh shoot. Too much time enjoying nature," Bugz said, still lost in the virtual scene. "Where are these losers coming from?"

A murder of crows scattered from a poplar tree to her right. Bugz turned and held her breath. No movement, no sound, not even a reflection across the water.

Bugz unholstered a flare gun from her thigh and fired it high above the offending tree. The flare exploded like a shimmering orange firework and illuminated hundreds of Clan:LESS soldiers struggling to stay hidden behind cloaking shields. These handheld defenses actually hid the soldiers from Bugz, for the most part. However, her flare revealed scores of battle helmets, antennae, and scalp locks sticking out over the top of the invisibility screens.

"Formation 2-1-2!" A voice that sounded an awful lot like Alpha's rang out across the water.

"Oh, so they got formations now?" Bugz asked for the benefit of her fans watching along on the livestream. The flood of gifts appearing in her chat window acted as a visual laugh track.

She turned her canoe to face the oncoming attack. She could see the horde splitting into two roughly even groups, each circling along the shore in opposite directions, one to the south and one to the north. *Of course Alpha is coming back for more. A never-ending hunger.*

Bugz opened a screen to quickly show a video about Alpha's backstory for the benefit of her followers. Alpha's first clan had bullied him and, just like the runt of the litter, the experience soured him. You could see the resentment on his face in the video as he endured taunts and insults. Then the action cut to a replay of Alpha following his clan into battle. They were trusting him to protect their flank, but instead, he slaughtered each and every one of them. Alpha pillaged their weapons and resources. Bugz paused the video and zoomed in on the charred remains of his former clanmates, their faces frozen in horror at his treachery. She skipped ahead of the short work Alpha had made of the other clan they'd battled that day and watched the climax of the clip. Alpha, still unharmed in this playback, and spurred on by virtual adrenaline, slowly cut his own face with a hunting knife, leaving himself with his signature scar.

Bugz snapped the video window shut to face this scarred warrior and the clan that was not a clan.

CHAPTER 18

Feng battled to keep up with the crowd of centurions, marines, and orcs rushing to Bugz's southern flank.

"Lock and load!" came the order over their voice communication system.

Feng pumped the action on a super-charged shotgun, boarded a speedboat—one of fifty that launched from this shore—and headed for the armada of sturgeon surrounding a single birchbark canoe in the middle of the lake.

Another fifty speedboats and Zodiacs launched from the north shore.

Feng watched Bugz's livestream through his heads-up display. He heard her speak.

"Are these guys serious?" Bugz asked her fans. "Splitting up into two? Making each of their groups weaker? Just like Custer at Little Bighorn."

Feng muted her feed as Bugz knelt down in her canoe.

Suddenly, the sturgeon submerged themselves in the black water, darting away with shocking speed.

Seconds later the first sturgeon tore through the waters directly in front of Feng's speedboat. The monstrous bottom-feeder rammed the boat so hard Feng and the other five Clan:LESS warriors riding in it were launched airborne and fell in to the lake. Sturgeon now rammed Clan:LESS boats left and right, pitching dozens upon dozens of soldiers into the churning waters around them.

Alpha surveyed the damage from a dinghy that broke through the masses of sturgeon. Over voice-com he ordered, "Call in the second wave!"

Thirty-five elite Clan:LESS fighters jumped from a floating aerial platform high above Lake of the Torches and skydived toward the battle below. Their forms could be made out against the starry night sky.

CHAPTER 19

"Come on, where are you?" Bugz, still kneeling, whispered into the waters around her canoe. "Come to me. Don't worry, they're not going to find it. I need you now."

Bugz heard the roar of motorboats closing in around her. A fiery arrow pierced the bow of her canoe and flames engulfed the birchbark, a remarkably flammable material. Bugz broke the first rule of canoeing by standing up in her vessel. In every direction she turned, she stared down barrels of guns drawn and trained on her. They would fire in an instant.

"Mishi-pizhiw, now!" she screamed.

An observer able to parse the nanoseconds from the milliseconds would've seen the individual laser beams, bullets, fire-tipped arrows, and buckshot closing in on Bugz from nearly every one of the 360 degrees around her. As the fire raced toward Bugz, the giant underwater serpent she'd summoned shot up from the depths below, smashing the burning canoe to embers and tossing the young woman high into the air. Bugz grabbed the supernatural being's horns as it continued to climb in altitude. The gunfire and projectiles rammed into the monster's ascending body and ricocheted off like sound waves from a metal wall. The beast appeared impenetrable.

Feng now thrashed in dark waters among many of his clanmates. He reached for an outstretched hand and looked in fear at Mishi-pizhiw. A comrade dragged him aboard a Zodiac and he lay on his back for a moment watching Bugz's giant snake. He shook his head.

The paratroopers still hurtling down toward the lake opened fire on Bugz and Mishi-pizhiw as they came within a few hundred yards of the still-ascending pair. While Mishi-pizhiw's body may have been nearly bulletproof, his face was not. The fire from above affected him: it slowed his climb, forcing him to turn back toward the water's surface. Mishi-pizhiw's dark body dove deep into the waters, with Bugz hanging on like a lamprey on a shark.

The Clan:LESS skydivers tore into the water headfirst, each wearing a diving suit capable of withstanding the tremendous force of their mile-high plunge. The thirty-five hunters kicked their webbed feet furiously as they chased Bugz and her partner into the deep.

In the depths of the water, like the gates of Atlantis, a ring of stones sat in a rough arrangement on the lake's floor.

"Sir, I think we've got eyes on it. It must be her power source."

"Mark its location," Alpha shouted through the voice-com. "Maybe we've finally solved the mystery. The secret source of Bugz's power."

By now Bugz had hacked into their communication system and was eavesdropping.

"Do you copy?" Alpha's voice asked.

Silence.

"Divers, do you copy?"

Static.

"Copy?"

In the depths, emerald light caught the lead diver's lifeless 'Versona, trapped in Mishi-pizhiw's jaws. The saber-toothed snake played with it like a cat with a mouse.

"That's enough!" Bugz yelled, struggling to hold on. "He's finished!"

The thirty-four remaining divers, now swimming furiously to the surface, pointed their guns back down into the depths and fired toward Mishi-pizhiw's head.

Mishi-pizhiw unclenched his jaw and virtual blood clouded the waters. He and Bugz chased the divers to the surface, picking off three more along the way, before turning away.

CHAPTER 20

Feng helped two divers board his boat as the other surviving SEALS scrambled onto watercraft around them.

"Should we head for shore?" The question came over the Clan:LESS voice-com.

"No!" Alpha shouted back. "We stay and fight!"

Feng looked around. Clan:LESS's chances of winning this showdown seemed to be slipping further away by the second. The last beatdown they'd received from Bugz had made it difficult to recruit more soldiers. With that livestreamed thrashing viewed by every serious gamer alive, and by tons of noobs too, Clan:LESS's reputation had taken a nosedive. If they needed to rebuild their army a second time, they'd either have to leave many spots empty or accept much-lower-caliber recruits. But the boss had said what he'd said. Feng sighed.

Mishi-pizhiw jumped up from the water like an orca

catching a seal and tore through a speedboat on the opposite side of the armada from Feng. Bugz, now straddling the beast's back like a mounted warrior, fired her machine gun into the waters around the shattered vessel; a cloud of gamertags rose to the heavens in response. She showed no mercy.

Feng fired listlessly at Mishi-pizhiw, who bounced from boat to boat like a wakeboarder slaloming from wave to wave, leaving destruction in his path. Bugz picked off any clanmates who'd survived the initial onslaught. Fifty more gamertags rushed skyward.

From the sky, the Thunderbird descended like a screaming eagle and rained lightning bolts down on the remaining Clan:LESS watercraft.

"C'mon, this is getting ridiculous," Feng said to the centurion beside him. He reloaded his weapon and fired several blasts at the Thunderbird above. "Let me guess, this one's bulletproof too?"

Bulletproof, perhaps, but the physics of the blasts forced the bird to change her flight path.

As the Thunderbird arced along her new course, she caught sight of Mishi-pizhiw. Without seeing Bugz on board, the bird fired several lightning bolts at the underwater beast, striking him.

"Watch out! I'm right here!" Bugz yelled skyward.

As the Thunderbird came within striking distance, Mishi-pizhiw lunged forward like a cobra attacking its prey and snapped at the taloned feet of the Thunderbird.

Bugz scrambled to keep her grip as the sudden movement nearly threw her into the water below.

"Could you guys *NOT*!" she screamed.

"What the heck is going on?" Feng asked of no one in particular.

"Looks like sibling rivalry, fighting for mom's attention," the centurion quipped. "I think the bottom line is, we've got an opening to get the hell out of here."

"Retreat!" came the call across the voice-com. "We will win . . . later!"

"Finally!" Feng spun the motorboat's steering wheel and headed for land.

As the dwindling fleet of Clan:LESS vehicles sped toward the nearest shore, the horned serpent and the thunder-being turned to give chase, one from the air and the other from the lake. They took turns striking down the remaining vehicles until there were eight, seven, and finally just six left.

Alpha's ship ran aground first. He and the others spilled out and ran for the helicopter gunships waiting to ferry them to safety. Four other boats crash-landed immediately after. The occupants flooded out but landed in the crosshairs of the Thunderbird and fell to her.

Feng's boat was last. He and his crew jumped off in the shallows of the lake, running through the mud after Alpha and the others, who waved them on. Mishi-pizhiw leapt from the waters, transforming along the way into his panther-like land form, and attacked the centurion. With

Bugz still riding on his back, Mishi-pizhiw broke the Roman warrior's neck and tossed him far away into the lake. A gamertag rose solemnly in the background. Four additional clanmates were dispatched with similar ease.

Feng fell into the mud and scrambled forward toward the choppers. It was pointless. Mishi-pizhiw caught him without effort.

Feng felt the beast's massive paws pinning him on his belly, almost crushing him in the process, before flipping him onto his back. He saw Bugz on the beast's neck, holding onto her pet's head. As the cat's giant fangs came within inches of Feng's face, Bugz paused. A glimmer of recognition flickered across her eyes.

Feng looked up beyond the beast about to devour him and stared into Bugz's face. He finally realized where he'd seen her before.

"Bagonegiizhigok," he mouthed.

"Feng from homeroom," she whispered.

"Triggered."

Mishi-pizhiw growled.

"Let him go," Bugz said.

Freed from the beast's mouth, Feng tore off through the mud and climbed the rope dangling from one of the remaining helicopters.

He collapsed on board. Even from one helicopter over, he could see the look of supreme disgust on Alpha's face. Feng wasn't sure if his clan leader was upset with the outcome of the battle, or by Bugz's mercy. A sense of dread overtook Feng as he thought about what had just happened—though no one in Clan:LESS would've understood why, they'd all seen he shared a connection with their mortal enemy, and he'd not disclosed it to them.

CHAPTER 21

As the Clan:LESS helicopters buzzed off like a ragtag group of dragonflies, Bugz climbed down from Mishipizhiw before he dove back into Lake of the Torches. She tore a strip of bark from a birch tree and threw it onto the water, where it promptly grew into another birchbark canoe. She climbed aboard, and as she began paddling again through the shimmering midnight waters of her lake, she re-engaged with the fans in her chat window.

"SnipesForDaze: Wow, you were right. That did turn out like Little Bighorn."

"Yeah, except Custer didn't survive," Bugz responded dryly. She disappeared into the virtual night.

CHAPTER 22

"And remember to keep a safe distance of at least six feet from each other." The intercom blared pointlessly as Bugz scanned the crowded school hallway. With home-room starting in a few minutes, students packed close together for one of the few times of the day before they all scattered to different parts of the school, or even home if they were lucky enough to live close by.

"Bugz?"

She turned to find Feng running up the hallway toward her, a book bag slung over one shoulder. Before she could pretend not to see him, the Clan:LESS follower had caught up to her.

"Wow, I can't believe I didn't figure it out sooner. I must be the only person at school who didn't know Bugz was short for Bagonegiizhigok." Feng raised his phone and saw her world-famous 'Versona staring back at him. He nodded his head in satisfaction.

"You must not be as smart as I thought you were," Bugz said, attempting a joke as she started to sweat. She imagined Feng comparing and contrasting her perfect Floraverse figure with her real-world body, and everything she disliked about it. She smiled nervously as she fretted about what his clanmates would say if they found out how she really looked.

"I deserve that," Feng said with a laugh. "I mean, it's so obvious, right? Bugz—Bagonegiizhigok. Plus, you're a celebrity. Your face even looks exactly the same."

Bugz felt a small sharp pain to the heart. *My face, but not my body, right?* Feng carried on talking. She studied his face for a reaction. Nothing. She played up her pained expression a bit more. Still nothing. He blabbed away, looking at her 'Versona through his phone without making eye contact or noticing her body language. Bugz often tried to convey her feelings to people she knew with thoughts instead of words. Quite often, like at this moment, the practice left her disappointed.

"Honestly, I thought you were just pretending not to know who I was just to make a good impression," Bugz said. She wondered if he was just trying to befriend her to gather intel for Clan:LESS. She eyed the main doors of the school down the hallway.

"I had no idea." Feng shook his head with a grin. "When I first met you, I didn't pull out my phone to check out your

'Versona. Thought it'd make me look too presumptuous."
The automatic translator on Feng's phone hadn't quite
chosen the right word.

"Well, most people who are nice to me either want
to get a selfie together or ask to borrow some money,"
Bugz said. She raised her phone and noted how similar
the real-world Feng looked to the Floraverse Feng. His
chest and arms were thicker in the 'Verse; otherwise, his
face was the same, his hair was the same, and his waist was
the same size. Her eyes found his again. "Wait, you're not
going to ask me for money, are you?" Bugz smiled at her
own joke. "Because I don't have any. My parents make me
leave most of it in the Floraverse for when I turn eighteen
in a few years."

"Wait, what? Are you serious?" Feng followed Bugz
to their classroom. "If I had the money you do in the
Floraverse, I would cash out and do school on a beach in
Macau or something."

"You sure you're not trying to ask for money?" Bugz
couldn't shake Feng's earlier offhand remark from her
head. *He probably wasn't even thinking about my weight*,
she tried to remind herself. She thought again of
Clan:LESS and felt forced to take a deep breath.

As they rounded a corner, they bumped into Chalice
and Stormy, both of whom were using their phones as
mirrors to check their makeup before class. Feng knocked
Chalice's phone to the ground and a thousand spiderweb
cracks exploded across its surface.

"Sorry," Feng muttered quickly. A worried look overtook his face as he picked up the broken phone.

"Gimme that!" Chalice snatched the device from Feng's hands. She looked at him as though he'd just dropped a baby on the ground. Feng said nothing. She looked to him and asked, "What the hell?"

Feng paused. "Sorry. It was an accident. I'm . . . I'm sorry."

"Sorry? That's all you got?" Chalice scoffed hard, exaggerating her reaction. She studied her reflection in the broken mirror she held. The screen glitched out a few times and finally died, leaving Chalice looking at her hands through a shattered piece of glass.

"Loser!" Chalice shouted at Feng. When his presence didn't magically evaporate, she flew into a rage and shouted again. "Friggin' Patient Zero! They shouldn't have let you into this school. Shouldn't you be in quarantine or something?"

"He said sorry," Bugz spoke up. "You don't have to be racist."

"I'm not being racist—it's true." Chalice's hate exploded in all directions. "Every single pandemic over the past two decades started in China. Every single one."

"That's not true," Feng stammered. "That's. Not. True."

"I can't understand you without my phone translating. You. Broke. My. Phone!" Chalice said loudly and slowly, as though it would help. "I've already replaced this

95

display twice. My dad is going to kill me!" Chalice's voice fell a decibel short of shouting.

Feng fumed.

"Wow, he looks really mad," Stormy said from behind her phone.

"What are you going to do? Cough on me? Where's your mask?" Chalice egged him on.

"Holy. Just relax, I'm sure he'll help you replace it," Bugz said.

"How do you know? You don't look so hot now there's no screen between us." Chalice spewed pure venom. "You're just a fat girl desperate for a boyfriend. So desperate you'll hook up with this piece of trash."

A crowd formed, made up of kids from both the nearby town and the Rez. They exchanged glances with wide eyes.

Bugz felt something welling up inside. In the Floraverse, she knew exactly how she'd respond. She pictured her 'Versona pulling twin swords from her belt as she backflipped high into the air, preparing to bring the blades down on Chalice. But in the real world of flesh, blood, and high-school drama, Bugz froze. Finally, she found words.

"You know, Chalice, it was a stupid accident." Bugz's arms burned as though she was cooking from the inside out. An image of her cousin Ally's arms flashed in Bugz's mind and she shook her head.

"Hey, leave my sister alone." Waawaate stepped in between the two factions. "Chalice, you can't talk to my sister like that. Apologize to her."

"Sorry!" Chalice soaked her words in sarcasm. She stared at Bugz, her expression still full of hate. "You're lucky your brother stands up for you," she said before taking one last look at Feng, "because your little boyfriend here sure ain't."

"I'm not her boyfriend," was the best Feng could muster. Bugz shot him a look of fury.

"Alright, that's enough. Let's get out of here," Waawaate said, putting his arm around Bugz's shoulders. His touch felt good and seemed to cool her arms. She wiped her nose with her shirt sleeve and walked with him to the outside doors. Waawaate motioned with his head for Feng to follow. Feng scanned the crowd of stunned teenagers, all of them livestreaming the aftermath of the altercation. Some started to offer commentary to their viewers.

CHAPTER 23

"Why they gotta be like that?" Bugz asked her brother.

"Well, did Stormy say anything mean to you?" Waawaate glanced at Bugz. "Anyway, you're right. That was super awful. I'll talk to them later. They should give you a real apology."

The trio walked to Waawaate's pickup truck, climbed in, and slammed the doors, Bugz riding shotgun and Feng in the back. Waawaate settled into his seat a little tenderly, his hip apparently still bothering him. "Let's go for a ride and chill for a bit. I'll ask dad to call the school." Waawaate texted with one hand and hit the vehicle's start button with the other. "Where do you want to go?"

"Take us to the bush."

Bugz could feel Feng watching her from the back seat as Waawaate slipped the truck into gear. As they left the school parking lot, Bugz pulled out her phone and peered into the Floraverse. She sought comfort from her super-natural friends. *I'll see you soon.* She realized the others in the truck were both looking at her.

"Thanks for having my back, Waawaate." Bugz sighed. She studied Feng through the rearview mirror. "Why did she have to talk about my weight? That's like the one thing I'm the most sensitive about. What a loser."

"She was trying to hurt your feelings," Waawaate said. "Probably insecure herself."

"I don't think you look fat." Feng tried to help cheer Bugz up.

"Really?" Bugz hungered for more.

"No, I don't think you're fat." Feng should have left it at that, but he tried to continue comforting Bugz. "I mean, we've all got some extra weight, right?"

"Extra weight?" *What is the matter with this guy?* Bugz thought. She felt the heaviness of the day dragging her down, taking the way she felt about Feng down with it. She tried to reassure herself that he was just a dumb member of Clan:LESS anyway.

Waawaate turned around to shoot Feng a look and turned back to the road. "No. I think his translator just screwed up. Right, Feng? What you meant was . . ." His piercing gaze still fixated on Feng through the rearview mirror.

"What I meant was . . . ," Feng said as Waawaate nodded his head, "that I think you look great." Feng continued, "You look really, really good." Waawaate kept nodding. "I mean . . ." Feng's face flushed. "You know what I mean."

"Thanks," Bugz said, a resigned smile on her face. "Even if my big brother is making you be nice to me."

Country music filled the cab as they pulled on to a dirt road and drove into the forest. The path wound deep into the woods until eventually they pulled up to a bush trail.

"Here we are," Waawaate announced. "You'll have to hoof it the rest of the way. I'll come pick you up later if you want. Just text."

Bugz jumped out of the front seat and walked to the trailhead. She turned back to the truck and raised her eyebrows to Feng. He removed his seat belt.

"Don't do anything I wouldn't do," Waawaate called after them, his tone mocking that of a concerned parent. He answered a video call on his phone from Stormy. As Feng closed the door, Bugz heard the start of Waawaate's conversation.

"What's up? Hey, you can't be mean like that to my little sister . . ."

His voice trailed off as the truck pulled away, leaving Bugz and Feng to walk along the path, their footsteps cushioned by red pine needles on the forest floor. Their eyes adjusted to the shade the forest canopy cast all around them. Bugz walked in the lead for a few moments until she turned to look at Feng, the renewed warmth in her eyes letting him know it was okay to join her. He caught up in a few steps and they walked side by side.

"That was messed up." Feng exhaled.

"I know," Bugz agreed.

"I'm sorry."

"Me too."

"You don't have to be sorry."

Bugz contemplated this before stopping to face Feng. "Then why are *you* sorry?"

Feng searched Bugz's face for a hint of what he should say next. He registered her facial expression, but it might as well have been written in the hieroglyphs of some long-forgotten language. And the automatic translator was no help for nonverbal cues.

I'm broadcasting this loud and clear, buddy, she thought to herself. *Read it in my eyes.*

"I'm sorry," Feng ventured, "that we almost got into a fight with those girls."

"Yeah, that was really too bad." Bugz turned and continued down the path. He didn't get it.

Feng ran to catch up with her and thought hard about what to say next. "I'm sorry I didn't stand up for you. Especially since you had my back about the racist stuff."

"Mm-hmm." Bugz nodded. *Please don't make this about you.*

Bugz could feel Feng's eyes on her as he did his best to keep pace with her. As much as he frustrated her, Bugz admitted to herself that Feng's clumsy attempts to make nice belied the picture she had of him as a member of a misogynistic neo-alt-right mob.

"What I'm most sorry about, though, is that when she called you fat . . . she hurt your feelings . . . when she was just trying to hurt my feelings." He sighed. "And I'm sorry I made you feel that way too."

Bugz felt herself become lighter. "It's not your fault," she replied, her eyes now smiling even as the stress still coiled around her spine. "It was an accident."

Bugz pulled out her phone and scanned the chat screen. She tapped out a few replies with her thumbs, her screen glowing an amber orange as she typed. Feng pulled his phone out too.

"Holy, what's going on?" he asked. His screen was filled with energy waves coursing wildly in random directions.

"Hey, weren't you still sucking up to me?" Bugz teased.

"Right." Feng chuckled, still staring at the amber glow from his screen. "It's just I think I saw this when I drove here, but then I couldn't find it again. It's like we're at the center of the universe or something."

"The center of the center of the universe," Bugz corrected him. "My universe, anyways."

"Wait." Feng stopped walking. "Did you bring me here to show me whatever it is that makes you super powerful in the Floraverse?"

"You think you're a big deal, don't you?" Bugz chided him. She bit her bottom lip. "It's a good thing you're cute."

Bugz surprised herself with the comment. The words felt dangerous and unstoppable as they escaped her mouth, but they left only warmth behind. She basked in that feeling. *Please don't ruin it by being needy or fishing for compliments*, she thought.

"What do you mean—" Feng began, but cut himself off. Bugz smiled as she watched him read the situation correctly for once and abandon whatever he'd almost said. "Thanks," he offered instead, and thought for a second before speaking again. "You're pretty cute yourself."

"You don't think I'm fat?"

"No," he said. "I think you're amazing."

They walked in silence, Bugz content to let the good vibes soak into the distance the earlier conflict had created. She closed her eyes and inhaled a deep, slow breath of fresh forest air. But instead of the relaxed feeling she usually got from being in the bush, a hint of concern crept in to her brain. The boy had been quiet for too long. What was he up to? She opened her eyes, looked down, and saw his hand reaching for hers.

"What are you doing?"

Feng's hand froze and found its way back to his side. "Nothing." He sounded like a kid caught with his hand in the cookie jar.

"You know, just because I said you're cute doesn't mean I want you to put your hands all over me." Bugz stopped. She didn't know if this was an overreaction, but she was a little freaked out things were moving so fast. Should she take back what she'd just said, or at least apologize for the tone in which she'd said it? She didn't know, so she simply continued walking.

After a moment, she realized she enjoyed a certain power over Feng. She tested the limits of this new feeling by lording it over him as she strode ahead. She grinned as she looked down at her feet. She was leading and he was following.

CHAPTER 24

Bugz ran up to an old chain-link fence whose posts sank lazily into the forest floor. In one fluid motion, she jumped onto the fence, pulled herself to the top, and vaulted over to the other side. For that briefest of moments, she looked exactly like her 'Versona. She turned to see Feng climbing the fence and trying to look cool while doing it. She smirked.

The square-fenced perimeter defined this forest clearing. Inside sat a dozen trailers. Fragments of painted words like *TCO* and *ISO-3* peeling from their walls bore testament to their past usage.

Bugz walked up to a trailer and forced the door open with some effort. "C'mon." She motioned to Feng as she disappeared into the shadows. Inside the trailer she pulled her phone out, the amber screen illuminating the space around them with an eerie glow. Feng followed closely behind her and pulled his phone out too.

They walked down the narrow hallway and saw piles of file folders scattered everywhere on the floor. Black mold swept across the debris, slowly claiming new territory. Further into the trailer, they passed an administration desk and a bank of cubicles. A giant banner along one wall read *Wash your hands!* A matching sign on the far side spelled out *N100 masks required.* Bugz and Feng climbed up on the desks and made a game of jumping over the cubicle walls. They arrived at the end of the trailer. It joined another, and Bugz forced this new door open. She and Feng stepped in and stopped still in their tracks. This room never ceased to amaze Bugz.

Rows of hospital beds lined the trailer on both sides, each with racks and dollies where medical equipment had clearly once been installed. Dangling cables and wires suggested the equipment had been removed very quickly. A ventilator tube snaked out onto the floor from underneath the closest bed.

"You know what this place is?" Bugz asked.

"Let me guess." Feng sounded awestruck. "This is where your people did isolation in the 2020s during the pandemics."

"Bingo." Bugz stepped forward slowly. "They called it the farm. 'Get sent to the farm, you don't come back,' they said."

"Back home, they built massive hospitals in some cities overnight. But I've never seen anything like this."

"There's pictures and videos showing this room full of our people. Everyone hooked up to ventilators. Emergency staff and military personnel flown in to run this center. Complete separation from the community."

"It's amazing your government let it get this bad. Our government isn't perfect but the party was able to control the pandemics quickly, without mass deaths."

"You believe that?" Bugz scoffed. "And let me guess, that's proof democracy is overrated, right?"

"Well . . ."

"Well, don't be so gullible. Some democracies beat the pandemics too; the problem we had here were the leaders at the time." Bugz shook her head, before motioning Feng on. "Anyway, the other trailers are more like dorms, where the people who weren't as sick stayed. Separated from their families."

"There's a really spooky vibe in here."

"People died."

"How many—"

Suddenly, a ventilator tube came scurrying across the floor at them. Bugz jumped and screamed. Feng jumped higher and screamed louder. Before Bugz could scream a second time her phone's light flashed off the eyes of a squirrel. The vermin scurried away to the wall, dragging the tube behind it.

Feng and Bugz looked at each other for a breath before bursting out laughing.

"Oh my god, I was so scared," Feng roared.

"I know, so was I!" Bugz shook her head as a belly laugh took over her body. "But I wasn't like you. You were all 'AHHHHHH!!!!'" Laughter consumed her.

"Oh yeah, like you were any better."

Bugz couldn't stop laughing.

"Okay, come on. Stop now."

"I can't help it. You should've seen your face."

"I get it. I was scared."

"That was too good." Bugz started walking to the far end of the trailer again. "Too bad I didn't catch it on video. I could post it in your Clan:LESS group chat." Feng did not smile but moved to catch up with Bugz. As though governed by an unspoken deal, the two of them walked closer together as they made their way down the aisle between the beds. "We used to come run around here as kids when we'd sneak out of our houses at night."

"Wow, you guys were bad."

"No, we weren't bad. That's just how it is on the Rez." Bugz smiled at the memory. "We'd come here after dark and run around and say, 'You're gonna catch SARS-3 if you touch the floor.' Then we'd jump from bed to bed and slide on the machinery racks like skateboards."

"That's terrible." Feng smiled nervously. "I mean, sounds fun . . . but there's such an eerie feeling in here."

"It was fun." Bugz shut her phone off and turned slowly to Feng, a deadly serious look on her face. "And guess what?"

"What?" Feng sounded scared.

"There's the squirrel!" Bugz yelled. Feng yelped. "Your best friend!" Bugz pushed Feng out of the way and sprinted back to the front door. Feng followed closely behind her. Neither stopped running until they'd left the trailers, cleared the chain-link fence, and run a hundred yards back down the bush trail.

CHAPTER 25

Feng caught his breath as he and Bugz slowed to a stroll.

"I showed you something cool," Bugz said. "So now you have to tell me something."

"Okay." Feng hesitated. "Shoot."

"Why are you part of Clan:LESS?"

"Because they're the best. Everyone wants to be a part of Clan:LESS."

"I don't."

"But you can't." Feng sounded defensive.

"Even if I could join your little boys club, I wouldn't. It's just a bunch of losers who try to make themselves feel big by putting other people down."

Feng noticed Bugz attempting to compose herself. "Everyone's so sensitive now," he said. "We're just having fun."

"Sensitive? Meanwhile, you're the ones who act like the biggest victims of all. As if men have it so hard. It's gross."

"It *is* hard to be a man now," Feng said. His shoulders felt more tense than usual.

"Even if you believe that, why join them?" Bugz angled her head. "Clan:LESS is the worst of the worst of the neo-alt-right. You make it impossible for women to play the game. You harass us, kill our 'Versonas, say gross things about us. I only survived because I can beat you."

"You didn't beat us. We're regrouping."

"Oh, give it up."

"Clan:LESS isn't all bad."

"It doesn't even make any sense that you joined them in China."

"Now you're being racist."

"They're white supremacists!"

"No, and you're being racist for assuming someone in China can't join this global movement." Feng replayed in his head all the times his clanmates had said racist things to him or in front of him, while Bugz stood by him, silently. The changing light indicated the sun was past noon somewhere far beyond the trees. Feng snapped out of it. "Well, maybe some of them are racist, but that exists everywhere."

"No, it doesn't."

"Well, that's just a few bad apples. Our real mission is to teach men to be strong."

"Real strength is kindness, it's compassion, it's caring about how other people feel."

"Look at history. For a long time China was weak, but now we're strong—the most powerful country in the world. And the West: first it was strong, but then it started apologizing for itself, and now it's in decline. So maybe being a man, or being strong, is due for a comeback." Feng's appearance conveyed his conviction. "That's what Clan:LESS is."

"It just seems like overcompensating. Seriously, would anyone ban women if they weren't afraid of them?"

Feng thought maybe Bugz didn't actually like him that much. Or at least not the way he liked her. She was really going after him.

"Well, talking to women has never been my strong suit."

They both exhaled. A crow called in the tree branches overhead.

"You know how to talk to me."

"What do you mean?"

"You know what I mean. You're just fishing for a compliment." Bugz paused.

"Well?"

"Well, grow up." She looked away.

"I like talking to you," Feng said.

"And I like it when you talk to me." Bugz's demeanor softened. "There."

"Hey." Feng stopped and took Bugz's hands in his own. "We're getting caught up on the wrong thing when there's something way more important I want to tell you."

"Yeah?" Bugz looked back at him expectantly.

"Yeah." Feng broke into a grin. "The squirrel's still right behind us!"

Feng took off running and Bugz gave chase for a few dozen yards. She caught up to him and gave him a good-natured push on the shoulder. They walked together.

"So, you gonna tell me your other secret now?" Bugz asked. Feng stayed silent. "Why did you leave China if you love it so much?"

"You want the long answer, or the version I tell everyone?"

"Tell me whichever one is true," Bugz said with a smile, "but make it snappy."

"Well, I was doing some work for the government. Volunteering, I guess. Going after people online, comment sections, you know."

"Sounds like real tough guy stuff."

Feng shrugged. "They had it coming. There are a lot of extremists where I lived in Xinjiang."

"Wait, is this where those children are being taken away?"

"Yeah, well, I'm one of them. I'm Uyghur."

"Whoa, I had no idea."

"Yeah." Feng paused before deciding to bare some of his past to Bugz. "But some people can't let go." He sucked his teeth. "When I was little, the government took me away from my family." He sighed. "I went to a boarding school, got educated, and left the old ways behind."

Bugz was silenced. Feng heard crickets striking up a chorus. He watched her throw a stick she'd been playing with to the ground. "They did that to my great-grandparents here too. They were taken to residential boarding schools by the government." She breathed deeply. "They hated it there." She looked to Feng. "How do you feel about the one you went to?"

"Honestly? It was tough." Feng found trust in Bugz's eyes. "But I think it was good. We had to change, get with the times of today."

"But it's wrong to take kids away like that," Bugz said. "What they did here was called genocide. Cultural genocide, they tried to destroy our identity."

"I know who I am."

"Do you?"

"I think it's different. You folks didn't want it. So it was wrong. But after I learned about the majority Chinese way . . . I guess I chose it."

"What about your parents?"

Feng shook his head silently. They could hear a cricket warming up as though preparing a song. Feng watched Bugz reach for his hand. Her touch sent a tingle running through his body. He thought of his mom. He wondered why she hadn't reached out like this, like she used to when he was a little boy.

"I'll show you all you need to know about my parents." Feng opened a video on his phone. It showed a young Feng in what appeared to be a principal's office. Feng narrated the conversation for Bugz.

"See, up to this point, I was resisting, telling them I wanted to go home. And this is where the headmaster explained there was no home to go back to. My mother and father didn't want me." The boy on the screen lowered his head to cry. "Right there, that's when he told me my parents could've brought me home within a week if they'd only rejected their stupid beliefs." He stared at the video as the corners of his mouth drew downward. "What kind of parent puts anything ahead of their kid?"

"I'm sorry."

"Now you know." Feng shook his head. "There is no 'going back' for me. Only forward. I saw Alpha livestreaming a few weeks after that video was taken and the rest is history."

The crow called out a few more times and flew off.

"So what was the problem?" Bugz asked. "You sound like a good little boy. Believing everything the government told you."

"I guess I was. But Clan:LESS became really important to me too. At least until you got me in that first battle." Feng chuckled and glanced at Bugz, who smiled. He continued. "Anyways, long story short, they can't monitor you in the 'Verse like they can on other digital platforms, so they think you're suspect. They asked me to quit Clan:LESS. I didn't."

Bugz was silent. A slight breeze rustled the leaves at the edges of the clearing.

"I guess as much as I love my country, I love Clan:LESS more. They were there for me." Feng looked off into the woods.

"That's messed up." Bugz let go of Feng's hand. "That's why I showed you mercy? So you could run around with people who deny my right to exist?"

Feng had no answer. He could only watch as she walked toward the mouth of the bush trail where Waawaate had dropped them off.

CHAPTER 26

Bugz heard Feng's loud footsteps behind her, seemingly crunching every twig and branch in the forest. *City boy.* She made no effort to slow down. Finally he caught up to her, almost out of breath.

"Bugz, wait," he said.

Her gaze met his. Bugz processed the color of Feng's eyes. Brown, though a lighter shade of brown than you might expect from someone with his shade of skin. Bugz studied the myriad amber and ocher striations that made up his irises. She thought of the massive nebulae where stars formed in the far reaches of the galaxy. She found herself thinking about her phone. She pulled it out and scrolled. "What?" Her eyes remained fixed on her device.

"Don't leave. I'm just trying to be honest. I figured you, out of anyone, you'd understand where I'm coming from."

"Anishinaabe people lost everything. It's a miracle any

of us survived. Our culture was on life support and I rebuilt it in the Floraverse, okay? And now you're telling me you love the one thing that can actually threaten all that."

"Well, like I said, there's more to Clan:LESS than that." Feng attempted a smile. "They put me on their streams when I was first starting and help me build my followers."

Bugz contemplated this. Followers meant a lot to her. "I'm really sorry for what you went through as a kid, I really am. It breaks my heart." The whirlwind of Bugz's emotions toward Feng began to settle.

"Thanks."

"You seem like a good person, Feng. But it's a little scary who you hang out with . . . and you've got this serious look all the time that makes it tough to connect with you." Bugz looked to her feet. "But I guess I am glad we came out here. I'm getting to know the real you."

Bugz looked up and found Feng's eyes just inches from her own. He'd stepped closer. She closed her eyes, and inhaled. Feng touched her face. Bugz opened her eyes and cast them downward, slightly disappointed.

"I know what it's like to search for something," Bugz sighed. "Believe me, I know." She allowed his hand to run slowly along her cheek. Bugz struggled to match the toxic things she knew Feng was a part of online with the side he was showing her now. "But you don't have to prove anything to me or try to be tough or anything like that." Bugz breathed deeply, sensing Feng's gentle touch, sensing the air filling her lungs. "Maybe everything you're looking for is right here." She exhaled. "And maybe what I'm looking for is here too."

"With me?" Feng's hand stopped and rested on her chin.

"Yeah, with you, genius." Bugz smiled and stepped back. "Do you see anyone else around? Is Clan:LESS hiding in the trees?" She shook her head, still smiling. Her joke masked her true worries about Feng's involvement with the clan, which still flowed through her thoughts like an undercurrent.

Still, Bugz felt calmer and more comfortable with Feng. Together they walked back to the Rez in the fading light, talking to and texting each other as the day became night.

CHAPTER 27

Feng woke to a buzzing feeling, sort of like a hangover. VR sickness. It hit him whenever he spent a lot of time offline. He looked around and realized he was laying in dirt. As Feng stood he saw other members of Clan:LESS welding broken vehicles together and stacking pallets of ammunition. After scanning the tarmac and the helicopters they'd escaped on not long ago, Feng turned to confirm the location of Alpha's bunker, noting the Ø painted on the building's side. He looked to the sky—two moons. This was home base, the Clan:LESS headquarters.

Activity pulsed across the compound: sparks flew from the salvaged vehicles and sweat poured off the soldiers running from one task to the next. Everyone rushed to get Clan:LESS back in fighting shape, or at least strong enough to defend itself should another clan raid the base. Feng found his clanmate Gym crouched beside a vehicle, tightening lug nuts.

"Can I give you a hand?"

"No," Gym grunted. "I got it." He stood and looked Feng over from top to bottom. "You been checked out a long time," Gym said. "You ain't been in the 'Verse since the battle."

"New school, new house." Feng rubbed the back of his neck. "I've got a lot going on."

"Word is you're on the run out there, maybe in trouble with the law."

"Who told you that?" Feng focused on making eye contact even as he dodged the allegation.

"I don't care, to be honest. As long as you carry your own in our missions, you could already be in jail in the real world for all I care."

This small validation filled Feng's heart for a moment. It helped him find the nerve to pitch a cover story for his next move. "Anyways, I think I'm gonna go forage. It looks like we could use some more resources to help with the rebuild."

"Forage?" Gym looked at Feng like he'd just spoken Klingon. "What the heck you going to forage? Our top priorities right now are to fix the gear, find new recruits, and stockpile ammunition—in that order."

"I just figured we'd need more wood to build structures for the recruits to stay in and food for them when they get here. Just want to work ahead."

Behind Feng and across the tarmac, Alpha watched the conversation. Gym made eye contact with his leader, asking for direction. Alpha nodded his head and motioned, *Let him go.*

"Well, I guess that makes sense." Gym's tone softened.

"Alright, then. Thank you, brother." Feng leaned in for a bro hug.

Gym cringed; Feng was trying too hard. "No problem," he offered.

As they patted each other's shoulders, he placed a tracking device on the back of Feng's collar.

In the distance, Alpha nodded his head again and walked away to inspect some more troops.

CHAPTER 28

From across the Floraverse, Bugz could see Feng in a small oasis miles away from the Clan:LESS base. He'd taken the precautions they'd agreed on—headed deep into the desert where they figured he couldn't be surveilled. He dropped to a knee, his face the picture of focus.

"I can hear you calling me." Her voice sparkled across his voice-com. "Here. Hitch a ride."

Storm clouds formed overhead and a Thunderbird swept down from the heavens. It snatched Feng up in its talons and rocketed toward the edge of the virtual atmosphere. Feng suspected his clanmates would see the bird hurtling through the stratosphere, but he didn't care. He figured even if they saw the bird, they wouldn't think it had anything to do with him.

The Thunderbird announced its arrival at Lake of the Torches with a scream. Bugz, Mishi-pizhiw, and the other animals gathered along the shore. The Thunderbird swooped down toward the lake and dropped Feng roughly on the ground. The bird glared at Mishi-pizhiw for a few seconds and took off.

"They don't like each other, do they?" Feng asked, attempting to break the ice.

"You made it!" Bugz greeted him with a hug.

Mishi-pizhiw dove into the lake and disappeared beneath its surface. Bugz and Feng watched the shadow of his form fade from view. It was a dark afternoon. The sky was covered with a purple and orange haze, giving the day an eerie feel.

"So, you want to learn how to be a Floraverse ninja?" Bugz teased. "I'll show you around."

"I've been here, remember? Twice!"

"Oh yeah." Bugz grinned as she scooped up a small red flower from the ground. "Didn't you leave with your tail between your legs?"

"Maybe someone let me leave because she couldn't stand the thought of living without me?"

Bugz forced a shallow laugh. "Don't flatter yourself. Anyways, don't share any of this with your stupid clan, okay?"

Feng nodded.

"Okay, check it out." Bugz closed her eyes, breathed deeply, and focused intensely. She held the flower up to the sky for Feng to see. The sun, emerging from behind the clouds, cast a golden light on everything around the lake. The flower turned toward the sun and back again toward Bugz. Suddenly another flower grew from the same stem, then four, then eight, then sixteen. Within a few seconds, thousands of flowers poured from Bugz's hands. When she threw the flowers into the air their petals collapsed in on themselves and re-emerged in duplicates and triplicates. As they continued multiplying, they clumped together and formed a massive red flower two stories high. This giant flower composed of smaller flowers turned, pulsating, toward the sun. The smaller flowers ran continuously down the surface of the giant like a waterfall as the bustle of activity continued to grow and grow.

"I prefer roses," Feng joked. He couldn't quite hide the impressed look on his face.

"Shut up, you'll make me laugh," Bugz said, her eyes still closed. "The Floraverse is powered by an engine that is modeled on organic chemistry, right? But it's also geometric. Everything is a reflection of smaller things. If you connect with the smallest life-forms, you can bring them together to form bigger ones."

Bugz opened her eyes and broke her spell. The megaflower collapsed, sending petals down the length of the shoreline. In an instant, the two were standing on a red-flower beach.

"Pretty cool. But I don't see how you beat Clan:LESS with that."

"And that's why I always beat you guys. Every. Single. Time." Their eyes met. Bugz suddenly felt nervous.

"You didn't beat us, it's not over. We'll win in the end."

"God. Typically neo-alt-right garbage. You can't admit defeat. Even though you claim to care about uncovering the truth." Bugz shook her head. "Weren't you trying to conquer this place?"

Feng paused and looked at Bugz's moccasins. "I guess you did win."

Bugz smiled.

"It's one thing to make flower crowns or whatever," Feng said, trying to downplay Bugz's mastery. "But how do you make things like the Thunderbird and the underwater panther?"

"Same idea. You can work with anything living in the 'Verse. You understand a cell or a microbe, that's the first step to creating an animal." Bugz put her hand on the earth and a star-nosed mole quickly appeared and ran up and onto her back. She let it run across her shoulders, and suddenly there were two moles running down her other arm. Soon there were four, eight, and sixteen moles scurrying on the ground. After doubling a few more times they gathered to form a massive mole, the size of a rhino, composed of thousands of little moles writhing and crawling on top of one another. "And creating an animal is the first step to creating something supernatural." The mole-king, still growing, burrowed into the dirt quickly. After a moment, it shot up into the air and flew far into the sky. As it disappeared from view, it exploded into dozens of stars, each of which became fixed and shone brilliantly against the sky.

Dusk approached. Feng shook his head as Bugz admired the mole constellation. "But it takes everyone so long to level up into the Spirit World," Feng said. "And even after that, it took me more than a year just to learn how to create a horse. It blows my mind you learned to do all this."

Bugz shrugged. As much as she was opening up to Feng, she still didn't entirely trust him. So she changed the subject. "Let's go for a ride." Bugz waded into the water. "And you have to swear not to tell your clan about any of this, okay?" She walked into the shallows up to her waist and dove forward. She surfaced a few feet away and rolled into a backstroke as she called Feng to join her. He offered his best slow-motion movie-style run into the water. *He's trying to look good for me*, Bugz thought. *That's cute.*

"Mishi-pizhiw!" she shouted.

"Is he coming?"

"He's already here." Bugz looked beneath the surface at the dark body below them. Before he could look down, Feng felt the lake bottom rising beneath his feet. "Hang on!" she shouted.

Suddenly the massive beast emerged and leapt out of the water. Bugz and Feng were tossed from the shallows into the air like children launched from their parents' shoulders. Mishi-pizhiw screamed at the sun and dove back into the lake.

Surfacing a hundred yards away, Mishi-pizhiw breathed fire into the sky several times to amuse them.

Bugz and Feng laughed and clapped their hands at his dancing dragon show.

Bugz looked to the sky and caught a glimpse of the Thunderbird flying overhead. She waved. The bird swept down screaming. It picked Bugz and Feng up and tossed them onto its back, and flung a few thunderbolts at Mishi-pizhiw for good measure.

"That's how we made the lake," Bugz said. "It was carved out of the landscape during a serious fire-breathing, lightning-crashing scrap they had a few years ago." Bugz wiped water from her eyes. "All the craters filled up with groundwater. And voilà. Lake of the Torches."

The Thunderbird took them flying low over the hills and treetops. Bugz and Feng squinted in the face of the tremendous air current streaming over the bird's back.

"Show me something cool."

"Like what?" Bugz asked.

"I don't know, more flowers."

Bugz closed her eyes for a moment. When she opened them, she turned to examine their flight path. A giant wave of flowers was closing in on them. It looked like a tsunami whose crest was about to envelop the Thunderbird. The bird looked back over its wings nervously. Soon the wave of flowers crashed up against it, but rather than dragging it to the earth, the flower tide pushed the Thunderbird forward, higher and faster. The bird squawked and flapped its wings in surprise. Bugz and Feng roared with laughter, deep belly laughs that came half from the bird's reaction and half from the feeling in the pits of their stomachs, like the feeling you'd get on a rollercoaster. The bird squawked until it steadied itself and learned to ride the wave. Eventually, it shook its head as though clearing its thoughts.

"Awww," Bugz said, petting the Thunderbird's head. "Did I scare you? I'm sorry." As she tried to reassure the bird, it looked away, like a child angry with its mother. "Aww, don't be mad . . . because that was nothing compared to this!"

A train of animals on the ground ran along below Bugz, Feng, and the Thunderbird. This pack of creatures could only watch in awe as the wave of flowers suddenly spiraled high into the sky. The seemingly endless trail traced a giant loop-de-loop before tightening rapidly into a smaller corkscrew shape. The Thunderbird jumped off the wave and banked sharply to the right, abandoning Bugz and Feng who landed on the flower tsunami and continued riding it by themselves.

"Guess she's had enough," Feng said, looking behind them.

"I guess so." Bugz smiled. She glanced down at the slim waist of her 'Versona. Shame crept back into her heart, into her mind. She examined the beauty all around her, the flora propelling her toward the heavens, the fauna running devotedly behind her on the ground, the boy she liked riding shotgun. In her mind, she knew she should be filled with joy. Yet something held her back. It weighed on her and prevented her from breaking into a full-on, teeth-baring, eye-squinting smile. Instead, she looked to Feng, and back to her waist. *What the heck is wrong with me?*

"This is awesome!" Feng yelled, smiling as the cork-screwing flower-wave hurtled back over Lake of the Torches. His laugh shook Bugz from her pity party. A smile found its way across her face.

"What?" Bugz shouted back.

"This is great!"

Bugz felt the virtual sun on her cheeks. She closed her eyes and shouted, "Onizhishin Anishinaabe Aking!"

"Onizhishin Anishinaabe Aking—my translator can't handle that!"

"It means 'Anishinaabe Country is beautiful!'"

"This isn't Anishinaabe Country! It's the Floraverse."

"This is how Anishinaabe Country *used* to be!" Bugz shouted back over a wide grin. As she yelled, something unlocked within her. "This is where I'm really me!"

Bugz meant it with every ounce of her being. In the real world, her culture was called backward and left for dead. In the real world, she was always too self-conscious to let herself fully relax. In the real world, she was a shy girl who ran away from problems. In the Floraverse, she'd recreated her culture as infinite and futuristic. In the 'Verse, she'd reimagined herself as confident and beautiful. In the 'Verse, she was fearless.

As they soared high above the majestic rocks and waters, Bugz fell in love with this feeling. Her heart swelled further as she started to feel like she'd maybe found a partner at long last. Not just a bot in the Floraverse . . . but a real live partner in Feng, another person who could see her for who she was and all she'd done. Bugz pushed her concerns about his membership in Clan:LESS to the side and smiled a smile she'd bottled up inside herself for years, perhaps since she was first formed in the womb. The smile felt good and brought warmth right down through her body and into her soul.

Bugz cried out again, "Onizhishin Anishinaabe Aking!"

The tracking device on the back of Feng's collar flashed, completely unnoticed by either of them.

Back at the Clan:LESS headquarters, Alpha, Gym, and a crew of soldiers watched the entire scene on a pop-up display.

CHAPTER 29

Bugz stared through her phone at the empty dinner table, toggling back and forth between the Spirit World, where her bot generated new animals to trade, and other random apps, waiting for something to catch her attention. She closed her eyes and saw nothing but darkness, save for a glowing rectangle in the center of her field of view where her phone had been. She reopened her eyes as Liumei and Feng walked in from the kitchen carrying several dishes loaded with food. Through the filter of the Floraverse, she again admired how much Feng's 'Versona looked like he did in real life. *He's comfortable with how he looks*, she thought. *Why not? He's cute.* Her eyes softened and her face relaxed into a faint smile.

"Thanks for joining us, Bugz . . ." Liumei paused, appearing unsure what to say next. "Is it alright if I call you that? Or do you prefer I say your full name . . . Bagon-ay—"

"Bagonegiizhigok," Bugz said to Liumei from behind her phone. She peeked over the top of her screen and examined Liumei's face . . . delicate features, for the most part. *She's pretty*, Bugz thought. "But it's alright if you call me Bugz. It's what everyone else calls me."

"Are you sure? You seemed to sit up a little bit straighter when you said your full name to me just now." Liumei's attention to detail was sharp. *Well, I guess so. She's a doctor.* Liumei continued, "To be honest, I'm still getting used to saying 'bugs,' but I'll get over it." Feng chuckled.

"Yeah, trust me, kids made a big deal out of it in elementary school," Bugz said. "They'd always ask if I had bugs, if I wanted Nix, or they'd say my first name must be 'sheehaz.'"

"She-haz?" Feng asked.

"Yeah, they were asking if her full name was 'She-has-bugz,'" Liumei said, plating the food. She gave her nephew a sideways look, as though skeptical of his intelligence for a second. "Listen, Bugz, part of my name translates to 'willow.' So I went by 'Willow' when I first got here until someone asked if it was 'cause I was skinny." Liumei shook her head.

Bugz couldn't help but smile at this. She decided she liked Liumei just a bit more for this confession of their shared experience. "My name means 'hole-in-the-sky' or 'hole-in-the-day.'"

"That's very poetic," Liumei said.

"Thanks." Bugz didn't know where to look. She glanced at her phone. "It was the name of a big chief back in the day. Our great-great-great-great-grandpa. He's the reason our family is called *Holiday*. When he registered with the government, they couldn't get his name right, so they switched 'Hole-in-the-day' to 'Holiday.' My parents wanted to honor him so they gave me the feminine version of his name."

"Impressive. So what does the *Bug* part mean?" Liumei asked.

"Nothing." Bugz knew she should say more. "It doesn't mean anything on its own, but it's part of the word that describes something having a piercing or a hole in it. And then *giizhig* means 'sky' or 'day' or 'cedar' in our language. Cedar is sacred to us and has a connection to the sky." Bugz's eyes darted around the table. "And the sky represents the day."

Liumei nodded thoughtfully. "I don't know how much Feng told you about why we invited you over, but it's the Dragon Boat Festival, which is usually a pretty big deal. And we kinda wanted to share some of our culture with some folks here because everyone's been so nice." Liumei looked to Feng, who only stared at his lap, before she continued. "Anyways, seemed like a good enough reason to invite you to dinner." Liumei glanced back and forth between the two teenagers again. "Feng, do you want to say anything before we eat?"

"Sure." Feng looked to his lap nervously. After a brief pause he spoke up again. "I was thinking about the adventure we went on in the 'Verse yesterday and it reminded me of part of a poem Qu Yuan wrote that I studied in school.

He's a poet with a connection to this festival." He cleared his throat. *"Ascending where celestial heaven blazed, on native earth for the last time we gazed."* As he finished, his face flushed, and he looked back to his lap. Bugz could tell this gesture meant a lot to Feng. Before she could speak, Liumei thanked him, and they dug into their meals.

"Fish balls, pork dumplings, *zongzi* . . . ," Liumei said, pointing at the different dishes for Bugz's benefit. "This is fried chicken." Liumei winked.

Bugz smiled and nodded. "And I know what this is," Bugz said, holding a piece of sweet and sour pork on a fork. "They have this at the mall." Feng and Liumei chuckled and a nervous silence settled over the room. Somehow the presence of a witness to their relationship made Bugz and Feng anxious. Bugz felt as though Liumei knew everything she and Feng had said to each other.

"Feng said you've been teaching him a lot about Anishinaabe culture," Liumei said between bites. "And you've done a lot of this in the Floraverse. That's pretty cool."

"Thanks."

"Hey, Bugz invited me to a sweat at her house tonight. Is it cool if I go?" Feng asked.

"Like a Sweat Lodge? Sure," Liumei replied.

Bugz looked around the table. "Do you want to come?"

"Wow, maybe. If you're just asking to be polite, it's totally fine. I've got some paperwork to do." Liumei smiled. It seemed to Bugz the smile was a bit forced. She figured Liumei felt a little sheepish about playing third wheel. Bugz looked to Feng for some guidance but he only scrunched up his forehead.

"That's okay. I was just being polite." Bugz didn't know why she withdrew her offer or why she now felt rejected. She felt a cramp in her belly.

They kept the stilted conversation going long enough to see them through the meal before clearing the table and each retreating behind their phones. Bugz and Feng jumped into the Floraverse, occasionally exchanging glances and the odd comment, while Liumei scanned medical notes.

A knock at the door summoned the dinner party out of its trance. Bugz rushed to see who it was. "It's my dad. He's here to pick us up." Bugz turned the doorknob as Liumei straightened out the shoes near the landing.

"Hey, Buggy!" Frank said, pulling his daughter in for a hug. "You guys ready to go sweat?"

"Hi, Frank," Liumei said.

"Hi, Dr. Turukun."

"Please, it's Liumei."

"Alright. Hi, Liumei. How were they? Didn't eat too much, did they?"

Bugz gave her father an annoyed look.

"No, it was great. They even talked to me a bit before they disappeared behind their phones."

"You were looking at your phone too." Bugz felt defensive.

"C'mon, Buggy." Bugz's dad nudged her. "Yeah, I know how kids can be. We had phones back in the day too. I'm guessing we're around the same age?" Bugz watched him smile when he saw Liumei nod her head in affirmation. "But it's nothing like it is now. Even in the heyday of Instagram and Snapchat, we didn't look at our phones as much as these guys do. Zombies."

"Well, what happens in the Floraverse is important to me," Bugz said.

"But is the digital world as important as the real world?" Liumei asked.

"The online world is more important to me than the real world." Bugz sounded serious.

"That's a shame, though. You're missing out," Frank said from the other side of a generational divide.

"Feng and I were just talking about the social media days and how it screwed everyone's brains up for a decade," Liumei offered.

"That and the social distancing. None of these kids grew up playing with others the same way we did," Frank added.

"No. We did all that. The difference is you lost your-selves in your phones," Bugz said almost plaintively. "We found ourselves online."

"We weren't so different, Buggy," Frank cut in. "I had a great Instagram back in the day. I was practically an influencer."

Bugz cringed visibly.

"Should we go?" Feng asked, ending the exchange.

"Yeah, we better get to it. Waawaate already has those rocks red-hot," Frank said. "You want to come too?" he asked Liumei. "Be a good chance for you to meet some other folks in the community."

Bugz noticed that whatever anxiety Liumei displayed earlier had evaporated. Liumei cocked her head. "Sure . . . what should I bring?"

"Well, bring a can of fruit as an offering, maybe. Bugz can help you with the rest," Frank suggested.

"Leftovers alright?"

"Sure. Buggy, you want to show her what to wear? I'll take this guy out to the truck," Frank said, nodding to Feng. "Don't take too long," he added with a smile. "I'll do my best to take it easy on him."

Bugz sighed and followed Liumei to her bedroom.

"So, what do you recommend?" Liumei said, leading Bugz to a closet bursting with clothes, most of it sportswear or professional-looking office attire.

"Grab a towel, and some kind of long dress. Maybe cotton?"

"I'm not really much of a dress-wearer," Liumei said, appearing self-conscious. She pulled out a cotton dress. It wasn't quite the right length, but it would do. "This okay?"

"Sure," Bugz said. She didn't know why, but she felt jealous of Liumei now that her dad had shown enough interest to invite her to the sweat. Bugz surprised herself at how annoyed she was. She suppressed this feeling and simply said, "Um, Liumei?"

"Yes, dear?"

"Have you got a tampon?"

CHAPTER 30

Bugz peered over the top of the star blanket she had wrapped herself in up to her eyes and studied the group of Anishinaabe people outside the low-slung canvas dome. They greeted each other with smiles and stood around restlessly, eagerly anticipating the moment they could enter the Sweat Lodge. The bent willow saplings framing the dome were said to hold up a mirror image of the night sky on the inside of the tarps. Bugz sighed as her father crawled into the sweat, that tiny recreation of the universe. She heard his muffled voice call the others to enter the lodge.

Bugz glanced at Feng. He stood in line behind the women, who crouched one at a time and crawled into the lodge. She'd never seen him without a shirt on before. He bowed his head and held both ends of the towel draped around his neck. He looked skinny, but not scrawny. She shook her head and looked away. Feng and the rest of the men entered the sweat. *Ladies first.* Bugz's thoughts dripped with sarcasm. Waawaate walked past Bugz, who didn't move to join the queue. She remained standing some ten paces from the lodge door, still hugging the blanket against the cool night air. Waawaate crouched near the doorway, listening to his father.

"Alright, son, bring 'em in," Frank grunted toward Waawaate. "Seven rocks." Waawaate nodded as he stood up slowly. Bugz noticed him groan as he straightened his legs. He shook one foot, paused, and limped like a dog with a porcupine quill in his paw for a few steps. By the time he picked up the pitchfork he'd corrected his stride. He tore apart the logs in the fire raging only feet from the Sweat Lodge door. He plunged the pitchfork into the glowing embers at the base of the blaze and pulled out a large rock, orange-red with heat. A blue-white flame slithered across its surface. Bugz watched the flame disappear as Waawaate carried the stone with the pitchfork, marched it toward the doorway, and slide it into the pit inside the lodge. "Aho, Nimishomis!" Bugz heard her father and some of the other men acknowledge the stone grandfather joining them in the sweat.

"Aho, Nokomis!" Summer and some of the other women acknowledged the rock as their grandmother. Bugz scowled.

Bugz set herself down in a camping chair with a long sigh, still wrapped in the blanket. She would spend the ceremony here. Outside. Excluded. Anishinaabe culture, like every Indigenous culture she knew, prohibited women from participating in ceremonies when they had their periods. Bugz couldn't believe this silly rule was preventing her from joining her friends and family.

The ceremony was supposed to be about healing, life, and the interconnectedness of all beings. All are related. Except for her, apparently. Or anyone else on their "moon time." And yet Feng, who knew absolutely nothing about this way of life, got to sit inside, front-row center, just because he was a boy. Bugz stewed on this slight. *Superstition.* Her frustration grew. She shook her head at the spiritual teachers—including many women Elders, including her own mother—who insisted on upholding this tradition. Sure, they'd dress it up in seemingly progressive talk, saying women on their "moons" were too powerful, too connected to the life-giving force inside them to participate, that their bodies would overwhelm the medicine men conducting the ceremonies. *There's something too powerful about women's bodies, alright.* Bugz knew it had nothing to do with magic, only fear. It was simply old-fashioned rule-making, condescension, and telling a woman what she could and couldn't do, as far as Bugz could tell.

She fumed. A ribbon of sparks exploded from the fire as Waawaate rolled a burning log over and pulled another red-hot rock from the center of the blaze. The pitchfork seemed to pull Bugz's anger out of her body for all to see. Her scowl matched the fiery intensity of the rocks the pitchfork retrieved. Everything infuriated her. She looked inside the door of the Sweat Lodge and saw Liumei sitting up very straight and looking incredibly focused. Bugz rolled her eyes. *Does she think this is yoga class? Oh my god, I hope she doesn't say "om."* To Liumei's left sat the woman who'd loudly reminded all the other women earlier that night not to go into the lodge if they were on their time. Women like her seemed to take special pride in broadcasting how much they knew about the culture—especially about all the protocols that kept women in "their place." This woman seemed to believe the stricter her scolding, the more virtuous she looked, and hence the closer to the Creator she became. *Traitor.* To the traitor's left sat Bugz's mom. Bugz looked away quickly and back to the fire. She seethed at her mother. How could her mom—their community's first woman chief in modern times, for crying out loud—think in such a backward way when it came to her body and what it did every month?

Bugz thought back to another night years earlier, when she'd listened to the fire crackle and hiss in the exact same place, as a young girl. Back then she'd sat on her mother's lap, the two of them bundled up together in the same star blanket Bugz now hugged. As they'd cuddled underneath the heavens, meteors, and northern lights, Summer told Bugz about the significance of the Sweat Lodge. It represented the womb of Mother Earth. "Those who go inside are reborn and come crawling back out of the ceremonial doorway renewed," Bugz's mother had said.

As she recalled this memory, it dawned on Bugz for the first time that her mom had sat outside the sweat with her that night because she'd been on her time. Bugz furrowed her brow. Her treasured childhood memory made possible only by their shared ostracism from the sacred gathering happening a few feet away. Bugz wondered which tradition she was helping to pass on. The Sweat Lodge ceremony? She didn't feel very involved with that ritual. Perhaps instead she was helping carry on the practice of keeping women on the periphery. She shook her head at the thought of women not benefiting from the symbolic renewal of the womb of Mother Earth because of the renewal of their own literal, real-world wombs.

"Stupid," Bugz said aloud.

"I know you are, but what am I?" Waawaate caught Bugz talking to herself. He grinned as he planted the pitchfork in the ground and climbed into the sweat. He pulled the canvas covers down behind him, plunging the interior of the sweat into darkness and leaving Bugz outside, completely alone with her thoughts.

CHAPTER 31

Bugz stared into the flames. The fire inhaled and exhaled momentarily with the wind. She thought of the time before the big bang. After a few breaths, she heard the muffled voice of her father praying in the Anishinaabe language inside the lodge. Bugz imagined herself inside the sweat with the others. She pictured the translucent red glow tracing the forms of the rocks in the pit and could practically feel the heat and the beads of sweat running down her face. With all of her heart Bugz wished she could be inside. She slouched lower into her chair until she was barely peeking above the top of her blanket, the rest of her immersed in the universe-like expanse of that old star quilt. After Bugz shifted in the blanket again, she could hear others taking their turns to pray. When they broke up the prayers with traditional songs, she hummed along. She knew every word, every melody. She knew them better than most of the men in the ceremony. Yet they were never asked to miss a sweat.

Bugz knew the ceremony wouldn't finish for a long time. Four rounds in total, yet the first had only just begun. Bugz thought of the feast to come after the sweat. All the participants brought food. She knew her parents assumed she would prepare it. Leave the food outside with Bugz and she will get the feast ready. They always expected women to take care of the preparations. Perhaps that's why some women always sat outside. *Free labor.* She thought for a second about cutting up the fruit and fry bread. Instead, she pulled out her phone and slouched even lower into her chair.

As Bugz peered through the glowing rectangle into the Floraverse, a growing realization of the silence inside the lodge crept up on her. She could hear no one praying. No one sang either. Something odd was unfolding inside the sweat. She put her phone down for a second and tried to eavesdrop. Nothing. She held her breath and focused harder. Finally, Bugz heard a whimper. It sounded like an animal, the sound of a young man trying to stifle his tears.

Feng. His turn to pray must've come, and now he couldn't respond. She'd seen this type of thing before. Somebody with emotions bottled up deep inside froze as they all came rushing forward inside the ceremony. This is why she was so upset at her exclusion from the Sweat Lodge—it had an undeniable power to it. She yearned so badly to be inside. Bugz resolved that when she grew older and took charge of running the ceremony, she would separate the superstition from the tradition, parsing the purity of the practice from the mistakes of the practitioners. If she ever grew to take charge of the ceremony, that is. Maybe her period would never end and she'd never get to sweat again.

The crying in the lodge grew louder. Bugz tried to imagine what might be making Feng cry: leaving his home behind; the racism at school; his parents. She wondered if he was thinking about her. She heard him cry harder still.

CHAPTER 32

"I don't want to talk," Feng said through a trembling voice. He felt suffocated by the heat and humidity of the sweat. His heart ached. His mind raced. He could see nothing around him in the darkness of the Sweat Lodge but still felt as though everyone inside was staring at him. Worse yet they were probably judging him for crying.

"That's okay, that's okay." Even with his limited English Feng could tell Bugz's dad was trying his best to sound reassuring. "Let it all out." They paused again before Frank recited an Anishinaabe prayer. "Aho! Baakinan!" he shouted in conclusion.

Bugz's dad and Waawaate shot their arms out under the door flaps and pushed the covers open. Light from the fire poured into the lodge's entrance just as surely as billows of steam rushed out of the doorway into the cool summer night. The rocks inside hissed loudly. No one spoke for a long time.

"How you doing, Feng?" Frank asked.

"Okay," Feng whispered, just loud enough to be heard over the cooling rocks.

"You know, sometimes when we have a hard time in a ceremony, it's because there are things going on in our life that we need to address," Bugz's dad said. Liumei nodded along. "No one here is judging you." Without Feng's phone nearby to provide automatic interpretation, Liumei translated Frank's words into Mandarin for her nephew.

"Do you want to talk about it?" Summer asked.

Feng paused long enough to see a torrent of images roar by his mind's eye: Xinjiang, his parents, his childhood mosque, the boarding school, the principal, young Liumei's tears, Bugz, Mishi-pizhiw, a Thunderbird's Nest, the ceremony he was now a part of. He cleared his throat and spoke in Mandarin. Liumei nodded along before translating again. "I guess he feels lost. Caught between a few different things . . . like different worlds. He thought he had it all figured out in China. Then he came here."

Feng thought of the Floraverse and the real world, of his Clan:LESS brothers. He thought of Bugz and himself, a young man and young woman. *Different worlds, for sure. I'm in the sweat and you're all the way out there.*

Liumei asked several questions in Mandarin, apparently anxious to help Feng verbalize his emotions for the others.

Feng felt nervous and hurried to answer, perhaps a little too quickly. He could see Bugz outside the lodge sitting beside the fire. He knew it was too dark in the lodge for her to be making eye contact with him but he could feel her gaze just the same. He felt she could tell he was uncomfortable and rushing his answers. Liumei spoke on his behalf. "Ever since he came here, he feels like maybe there's more to our family's culture. He feels it calling him."

He watched Bugz through the doorway. In the flickering firelight, he admired her beauty. He'd long ago concluded his people were backwards, but he'd come here to the Rez and met someone from an Indigenous background like his who was not ashamed of it at all. Instead, she wore her culture as a badge of honor and even turned it into something the whole world admired about her. As he pondered this, Frank, Summer, and Liumei exchanged glances.

Feng stared silently at the stones in front of him. He remembered sitting in the principal's office, hearing that he couldn't go home.

Bugz's mom spoke up. "You're walking in two worlds, Feng. Our Elders shared this teaching with us a long time ago. Walking in two worlds. One foot in the contemporary world and another foot in the traditional world. That's what I tell the kids in our community. We need the traditional footing to tell us who we are and the contemporary footing to get along in this world. I don't know what it's like to be you, but I'm guessing it's something like that. One foot in your culture, one foot in the mainstream. Does that make sense?"

Feng listened as Liumei translated.

"Frank, tell him about the Pipe and how it comes together," Summer said.

"Right." Bugz's father shifted in his place. "We've been given the Pipe to pray with by the Creator. The bowl of the Pipe is from women, from the earth, and the stem of the Pipe is from men, from the tree that grows out of the earth. But when you put them together like we do with the Pipe in ceremony, they form something new, something more powerful than either one of them were on their own." Frank paused for dramatic effect. "An Elder once told me you have to be like that. 'Be like the Pipe. Take the modern world and put it together with the traditional world and make something even more powerful than what was there before.' That's what she told me, and that's what you have to do too."

"That's beautiful," Liumei said from across the lodge, before turning and offering an interpretation to Feng.

Bugz's mother studied Liumei. She turned to speak directly to Feng. "It's not just a male and female thing. It's about two ways of life, two modes of being. Whatever they are for you, you have to put them together to make something new and more powerful. Everyone used to talk about reconciliation. This is it. Bringing things together to make something better."

Everyone in the lodge waited for Feng's response to Liumei's latest translation. He could sense it. So even as his mind raced with competing questions—*How do I reconcile my desire to live my life with the awesome power of the party? How do I fill the hole that my parents left in my heart?*—he instead said what he knew the others wanted to hear.

"Makes sense." While everyone in the lodge nodded in approval and assumed they'd done a great job in helping Feng bridge the Chinese, Uyghur, Western, and Anishinaabe ways of life, Feng's thoughts returned to something closer to his heart. *Mom and Dad.*

Summer nodded again. "Here." She took the eagle-bone whistle necklace from around her neck and waved it above the rocks. "I'm going to give you this to protect you while you're going through this challenging time. It's an eagle whistle." Summer handed it to Frank, who handed it to Waawaate, and so on down the line to Feng.

"Put it on if you want." Bugz's mom gestured as though she were presenting a medal to an Olympian. "You're supposed to earn that through an act of bravery or at the Sundance—our most powerful healing ceremony." Summer smiled. "I'm giving it to you now because it took bravery to show your emotions like you did tonight."

Bugz's father spoke again. "I'm going to sing a song. Blow on that whistle four times, and then I'll start." Liumei translated.

Feng blew the whistle softly, a light airy sound escaping the translucent yellow bone. Waawaate nudged him and whispered for Feng to blow harder. He pursed his lips and emptied his lungs. The tone flipped from that of a flute to the high, piercing sound of an eagle screaming in midflight. Three shrieks.

"Aho!" the others in the sweat exclaimed. Frank kicked off a song and all the Anishinaabe people joined in, punctuating the beautiful traditional melody.

CHAPTER 33

Though the hearts of everyone in the Sweat Lodge filled with feelings of warmth and happiness, Bugz felt cold. And it was not just because she sat outside the lodge. She did not sing along, even though she knew the words to the song. She sunk back into her blanket. *This guy cries and is treated like a hero.*

Bugz's jealousy roiled inside. There was more at stake here than just the eagle whistle, as beautiful as it was and as long as she had coveted it for. Bugz found herself wondering how Feng had come to deserve this attention from her parents. *It's because he's a boy.* Her jealousy blinded her to his suffering. Perhaps her ostracism justified her feelings.

She refused to look into the doorway. Instead, she compiled a growing list in her head of all the times her parents had failed to notice *her* suffering. Or her success in reviving their culture. *Why don't they make an eagle whistle for me?* She looked to Feng, who at that very moment had a tear running down his cheek as the others sang. *Lucky.*

Bugz wondered why she'd never received the motivational speech about walking in two worlds. She was the one who had to go back and forth between hating herself and feeling okay each and every time she picked up her phone. Skinny. Fat. Talented. Lucky. Virtual. Real. The song finished and everyone shouted in celebration.

Men just have to show up and the entire knowledge of all cultures of the world is handed to them. A woman like me can rebuild our entire civilization from scratch and no one even notices. Bugz turned her gaze back to the lodge, hoping her parents would see the mean look she was giving them. They didn't.

"Alright, we better close this door before it gets too cold in here. Waawaate, want to get that door?" Frank asked.

From where Bugz sat, it looked almost as though her brother had been shot by her father's words. As soon as Frank finished speaking, Waawaate collapsed and fell to his side.

CHAPTER 34

Waawaate's upper body sprawled out of the doorway into the fire's dimming light. His head rolled as though searching for help. Bugz froze. She could do nothing but stare into her brother's wide eyes. He appeared to stare through her and into the afterlife. She wanted to reach out and help him, but the sudden realization of her big brother's mortality kept her pinned to her chair.

"Son?"

"Is he okay?"

"What's the matter?"

Liumei's medical training kicked in as she crawled through the questioners and their chatter. She reached to check Waawaate's pulse and quickly confirmed his breathing.

Bugz remained still with fear as her parents spoke up.

"Leave him alone," Bugz's mother said.

"Yes, Liumei, back off," her father said sharply, before his voice softened. "When someone faints in a ceremony like this, we have to let them be. He could be having a vision."

Bugz read protest on Liumei's face but watched her relent after scanning the unhurried looks on the faces of Summer and Frank. "Okay," she sighed. "He's still breathing. I'm guessing he's not diabetic. He looks athletic. Is he epileptic?"

Her parents shook their heads. "He's having a vision," Frank repeated.

Bugz's concern for her brother transformed into anger at her parents for not doing anything to help him. She panicked at seeing the one she'd always assumed was invincible now appear so vulnerable. *He's not having a vision, he's hurt!* She added this moment to her list of grievances.

Feng spoke. Bugz didn't quite understand what he said, but she could see the effect of his words on his aunt. Liumei sat up straighter, effectively backing away from Waawaate.

Bugz wished for Feng to say something, anything else. She wanted the doctor to look at her older brother, to find out the problem, and to make him well again. She didn't want Liumei to go along with what everyone said just because of supposed tradition. *My brother is dying! Help him!* She wanted to scream.

Bugz threw the blanket down and rushed to her brother, who still lay in the doorway of the sweat. As she fell to her knees, she heard the others begin to chastise her.

"Bugz, you can't come in here right now," her mother's voice said.

"You can't come in the sweat on your moon. It ain't right," the traitor said. Bugz resisted the urge to scream. She'd heard enough from this woman already tonight. Surely even she could see that this wasn't a time for her posturing.

"She's on her time? She's going to make us all sick," one of the men exclaimed.

Bugz cradled her brother's head. His forehead felt too cold as she brushed the hair from his face. Tears welled in her eyes.

"Bugz, don't," her father said. "You know you can't come into the lodge, not even the doorway."

"Shut up!" Bugz shouted.

"Don't talk to your father that way," her mother scolded.

The traitor spoke up again. "You're disrespecting your body bringing yourself in here like that. Your body's too powerful to be around these men. Think of them. Think of their well-being."

"No!" Bugz spoke through tears. "I'm not going to listen to your stupid rules while you ignore my brother. Waawaate's lying here lifeless and all you can think about is the fact that I'm on my damn period." This silenced Summer, Frank, and the others. Bugz sobbed and bowed her head, covering her brother's face with her hair. Liumei bit her bottom lip. Bugz shuddered as she took a deep breath.

Waawaate stirred and blinked. Bugz felt his body come back to life as though he were returning from the promised land. He sat up and Bugz rubbed his back. Embarrassed more than anything, Waawaate assured the group he'd had no vision. Liumei recommended they take him to the hospital.

"After the sweat," Waawaate said. "We've got three more rounds to do."

"You sure?" Frank asked.

Waawaate nodded.

"Alright, at least let me grab the rocks then." Frank crawled out of the lodge to grab the pitchfork. He barely looked at Bugz as he passed. She seethed.

Bugz helped Waawaate back into the lodge and took a seat beside him. She could feel the stares of all the other Anishinaabe people in the lodge. The traitor's mouth was agape.

"I'm not leaving," Bugz said. She began to pray.

CHAPTER 35

In the depths of Lake of the Torches, the Behemoth targeted Mishi-pizhiw in his sights. The giant beast slept soundly, curled like a house cat. Still, the Behemoth knew he couldn't take his shot. His fire would bounce off the underwater demon's back and only awaken him in a foul mood. From there, based on how the last few Clan:LESS raids had failed, the Behemoth assumed he'd end up dinner for the pissed-off leviathan. He lowered his sniper rifle.

Since the last battle, when they'd marked the location of this stone circle, Clan:LESS had used the tracking device planted on Feng to fill in some crucial missing information. Most importantly, they knew when Feng and Bugz logged in and when they left their bots in charge. On a few occasions, when Feng left his 'Versona on bot mode around Bugz, they'd also watched her emerge from the lake with equipment and animals. They knew she made stuff down here. Not wanting to provoke another battle, Alpha sent the Behemoth on a solo mission deep behind enemy lines. But now, a giant serpentine panther lay in the way of him completing his task.

"I've got eyes on the nest," the Behemoth voice-commed back to Clan:LESS HQ. "But that giant water-cat is sitting guard on top of it. I need some kind of distraction. Otherwise, I'm bringing back nothing."

The voice-com went silent. As he waited for a reply, the Behemoth increased the magnification in his heads-up display by a factor of one hundred and studied the armor plating on Mishi-pizhiw's back. The cat shifted suddenly, apparently sensing the attention. He rolled over to face the Behemoth. His red eyes blinked twice quickly before he snuggled back to sleep.

The voice-com crackled as it returned to life, Alpha's voice unmistakable. "Okay, we've got a helicopter sortie incoming in T-minus one minute. They're going to lay down fire on some of the animals topside. We're hoping to provoke a response from the Thunderbird, lead the birds to fire over the water, and then, based on what we know of its behavior, we're hoping if some of the lightning hits the lake the big cat will rush to the surface to fight the bird. Capiche?"

The Behemoth sighed at Alpha's overly militaristic lingo. At times like this, the Behemoth sensed that maybe Alpha was just a wannabe. He stifled this feeling. "Yeah . . . capiche."

"Standing by?"

The Behemoth cringed. "Standing by."

Like clockwork, the telltale reverberations of gunfire shook the lake bed. A few seconds later, the low rumble of thunder overtook the gunfire. At this, Mishi-pizhiw suddenly snapped to and craned his neck toward the surface. A few more volleys of thunder and gunfire and Mishi-pizhiw darted toward the shallow waters.

"Okay, that worked. Keep 'em busy as long as you can," the Behemoth radioed home.

"We'll try, but they're barely hanging on already," Alpha replied. "10-4."

The Behemoth ignored this last message. He kicked his feet as fast as he could, swimming toward the nest. Once he'd arrived next to it, he tore the backpack quickly from his shoulders and unloaded its contents.

"How the heck does this thing work?" the Behemoth asked, forgetting his voice-com was on.

"I don't know, stand inside it and visualize something cool," Alpha suggested.

The Behemoth stepped inside the ring of stones tentatively, as though he might be electrocuted. As he realized no shock was forthcoming, he walked more casually toward the center. He held up a gun he wanted to upgrade. He closed his eyes. He scrunched his forehead. He opened his eyes only to find the same unimproved gun in his hands.

"Nothing happened," he said.

"Think harder," Alpha spoke through the voice-com.

"I am!"

"Try again!"

"I'm still trying!"

"Well, you're obviously not trying hard enou—"

The Behemoth muted his voice-com.

He held the gun up in the dim light permitted by the depths above—an old revolver he'd picked up from a cowboy early on in his career in the Spirit World.

Suddenly, a bolt of lightning from the battle above plunged through the water and struck the gun. The Behemoth's body coursed with electricity and charged the stones making up the nest around him. He felt the gun growing in his hand. He watched in amazement as the revolver grew and grew until it took the size and shape of an old automatic weapon called a Gatling gun. The Behemoth threw the Gatling gun to the ground outside the nest and set to work repeating his feat. With a second revolver in his left hand, he took an energy cannon and fired it directly at the nest with his right. Soon this gun also multiplied in size and power. The Behemoth repeated this process as many times as he could over the next ten minutes, creating a pile of supercharged weapons, including some innovations which were entirely new to Clan:LESS.

"Hey! Get out of there. Our guys G2G. They're getting smoked and they're worried Bugz is gonna log back in NE minute." Alpha's incoming text messages flashed on the Behemoth's screen. He turned his voice-com back on.

"Hey boss, got your messages. No problem. I got more than enough." The Behemoth gathered his haul and swam furiously for the shores on the far side of the lake from where the battle raged.

As he surfaced, a Clan:LESS helicopter scooped him and his loot up in a net and flew quickly back to headquarters.

"I'm back with the clan," the Behemoth radioed again. He examined the giant weapons he'd just fabricated. "I think we just changed the game."

CHAPTER 36

"Osteosarcoma."

Bugz, her mother, and her father all stared at Liumei.
The sounds of hospital machinery beeping and whirring
marked the time passing as they contemplated the news.

"Osteosarcoma?" Bugz's mom asked.

"Osteosarcoma," Liumei repeated. She wore a stethoscope and a lanyard around her neck. She looked to
Waawaate, sleeping in the hospital bed beside her. "It's a
form of bone cancer we sometimes see in children."

"Cancer?" Bugz's eyes welled with tears as her mother
turned to her father. He pulled Bugz's mother in. They
cried and held each other tight. It looked like all they
could do to stay upright. Bugz remained seated, looking
at her hands in disbelief.

Bugz watched Liumei struggle to find words. "I don't
want to say we're lucky—that's the wrong word. But

Waawaate did benefit from the fact the oncologist happened to be on-site today. Typically you'd need a referral and you'd have to wait quite a bit longer for this diagnosis."

"How did this happen?"

"It's difficult to say," Liumei said. "I'm not an expert on cancers. But what I can tell you from my conversation with the cancer specialist is that there is a mass on Waawaate's femur." Bugz followed Liumei's gaze down to the colored floor panels. "It's quite advanced."

"Is it terminal?" Bugz's mother asked.

"It isn't always terminal, depending on how early we catch it." Liumei swallowed.

"Well, what does that mean? What's going to happen?" Bugz's father prodded.

"We can't say for certain . . ." Liumei took a deep breath. "But like I said, the growth is advanced. Waawaate must've been sick for a long time and trying to tough it out. He would've felt a lot of pain. He must've been very stro—he must *be* very strong." Bugz processed Liumei's correction as the doctor spoke again. "There's always hope. There's always the people at the end of the bell curve who pull through."

Bugz nodded, biting her bottom lip in an effort to keep the tears from consuming her. "Can you cure him?"

"We'll try, and the oncologist wants a follow-up in the city—"

"Can you help my boy?!" Bugz's mom interrupted and raised the tissue in her hand to emphasize her desperation.

"We'll try," Liumei said, tears now welling in her eyes as well. "We're certainly going to give him every chance we can . . . I just don't want to give you any unrealistic expectations."

"Unrealistic expectations?" Frank's gaze fell to the floor as he mulled the words. Bugz's mother wrapped him in her arms again as if holding him together, and to stop him from sinking any further. Bugz ran to the door.

"I'm really sorry," Bugz heard Liumei say as she reached the hallway.

Bugz rushed to a private waiting room down the hall and sat on a plastic chair. She pulled out her phone and scrolled without paying attention to anything on-screen. Her mother arrived a few minutes later and turned the volume down on the television babbling aimlessly on the wall.

"Hey," her mother said.

"Hey." Bugz looked up and noticed her father entering the room. "So is it really going to take him from us?" She studied their faces and developed an instant fear of the truth, a truth she both wanted never to hear and couldn't stop herself from pursuing. Tears formed in her eyes.

Bugz let her mother pull her close. Her dad walked over and crouched next to the chairs where she and her mom sat.

"Tell me," Bugz said.

"We have to remember your brother's strong, very strong, and he's going to fight this. Remember your brother's a warrior," Bugz's mom said.

"Strongest warrior I've ever known," her father interrupted.

"Don't try and protect me." Bugz felt more tears pushing up from inside. "Just tell me the truth!"

"The doctors are amazed at how long your brother must've been fighting this—"

"I know, I heard. But is he going to die?" Bugz interrupted.

"Buggy, you know we're not supposed to talk like that," her dad said.

"Just tell me the truth. Is he going to die?"

Her parents' silence brought the truth closer to her. Bugz pulled out her phone and searched for "osteosarcoma," swiping through answers about mortality rates, symptoms, and treatments. The search results painted a picture of a particularly brutal road ahead, of the road Waawaate had already walked on for so long without telling anyone. Bugz sighed loudly and pressed her head against her hands, one of them still clutching her phone. A tear ran across the screen.

"Why?" Bugz asked. Both of her parents shook their heads. "So, how long?"

"Buggy, you know your mom and I raised you not to talk like that."

"Your dad's right."

"What can they do to help him?" Bugz's voice betrayed her frustration. Her parents looked to each other but didn't answer.

"What can they do?!" Bugz's face reddened with anger. She stomped to the door and threw it open. In the hallway her phone lit up with a video call from Feng.

"What's going on?" he asked. "Liumei said I should call. How's your brother?"

"I can't talk right now. I'm just leaving the hospital," she sobbed.

"Okay, well, can we talk—"

Bugz terminated the call. The heavy exterior doors of the hospital slid open silently at her approach and she ran into the twilight.

CHAPTER 37

When Bugz reached the mouth of the bush trail, Feng stood waiting for her on his bike.

"Hey," Bugz said. "How'd you know where I was?"

"How could I forget this place?" He examined the surroundings. "Scared the heck out of me." They both chuckled. "Besides, you told me you like to come here."

Bugz felt lighter. Feng remembered. Perhaps he knew her better than she thought. Maybe he really was more than just a Clan:LESS goon. She wiped her eyes with her sleeve. "He's got cancer."

"I'm sorry, Bugz," Feng said. He wheeled his bike closer.

"I searched it up online," Bugz replied. "I read up about symptoms and stuff. It said he might have a chance if they found it early . . . but they didn't."

Feng nodded his head and looked to the ground. Bugz buried her face in her hands. She didn't want Feng to see her cry. She wasn't sure why. Sniffing quickly, Bugz wiped her nose and cheek with her sleeve. "I was thinking about the fact that he passed out, though. And after watching some videos on that . . . he's really sick. I don't think he'll . . ." Bugz couldn't finish her sentence. Feng laid his bike down, hesitated for a breath, and then put his arms around her.

"My parents won't even tell me what's going on." Bugz pulled away from Feng and wiped her eyes again. "I mean, they told me he has cancer. But I know they know more."

"Maybe they don't know anything else."

"No, they do, that's how Anishinaabe people are. Proud. Private. Whatever. They won't tell me how long he has."

"I could ask my aunt. She's treating him, right? She'll know."

"Can you?"

Feng opened a video chat screen on his phone and reached Liumei, still at the hospital, stethoscope around her neck and a trace of redness in her dewy eyes.

"Hey, Feng."

"Hey, Auntie, I got Bugz here . . ." Feng tilted his phone to include Bugz in the video chat window. Bugz waved, sniffling again as she did.

"Aw honey, I'm so sorry. I just want you to know this isn't because of something he did or something he didn't do. This just happens sometimes."

"That's actually why we're calling, or sort of," Feng jumped in. "Bugz was wondering, or I guess we were both wondering, if you could tell us more about what's happening with him."

"I know you want to know. But you should really talk to your parents."

"I did," Bugz responded. "They won't tell me anything."

"Well, I should leave it up to them—"

"C'mon, Auntie."

"It's not my place to intervene in a family's business."

Bugz shook her head, more tears welling in her eyes. "Please!" Bugz's shouting seemed to hit Liumei hard. Bugz saw it on her face.

Liumei blinked once or twice on the screen. "Let me get somewhere more private." She ducked into what appeared to be a supply room. Bottles of disinfectant lined the shelves along the wall behind her. "Alright, so you know your brother has cancer. You know it's advanced, yes?" Bugz nodded over the video link. "Okay, so what else would you like to know?"

"How long does he have?"

"We can't say for sure. There are always exceptio—"

"Just tell me."

"Okay," Liumei hesitated. "A few months, maybe, but then again . . . could be less than that."

Bugz lost the ability to speak; she simply nodded at the image of Liumei she saw on-screen. Bugz avoided Feng's gaze.

"Thanks, Auntie," he said. "I'll see you later." Feng hung up and reached to pull Bugz close again. Leaning into his chest, she felt the eagle whistle rubbing against her arm. She reached into the collar of his hoodie and pulled the whistle out by its lanyard. She giggled through tears. Feng smiled.

"I like it," Bugz said.

Bugz fumbled with the whistle and brought it to her lips. She blew on it gently. A soft, hollow sound emerged from the thin bone cylinder. She smiled and sniffled before shaking her head. "Not supposed to do that," she whispered.

"What?"

"You're not supposed to whistle at night."

Feng listened. Bugz took his silence as an invitation to continue.

"They say if you whistle at night, the northern lights will come and take you away."

"Is that bad?"

Bugz looked at Feng as if he were an innocent child. She smiled just the same. "Yeah, it's bad. The northern lights are our Ancestors. They're dancing in the happy hunting grounds, in heaven, the Spirit World." She paused as she thought of the Floraverse.

"Spirit World, right?" Feng echoed her thought, though she wondered if the automatic translator had conveyed her true meaning. She stepped back, looked at Feng, and wondered how something as ugly as Clan:LESS, and everything they stood for, could befoul a place as beautiful as the Spirit World. She couldn't understand how a person who seemed as good as Feng could fall into their neo-alt-right orbit. She shook her head and stepped further away from him.

"Anyways, it's not good because we're supposed to keep the living and the dead separate. If you invite the northern lights here, you're inviting death. If they take you away, it means they take you away to heaven."

"I don't know. Why would you be afraid of your Ancestors or your loved ones? I mean, isn't that what we're hoping for—to be reunited?"

Bugz wanted to say yes, but tradition tugged her in the opposite direction. "I don't know." She looked to the rocks beneath her feet. "All I know is my brother is here now. And I want him to stay with us. Here. On this side." She studied the beadwork on the whistle again. "Waawaate. His name means 'northern lights.'"

"Really?"

"Yeah." Bugz started down the bush trail. She motioned for Feng to follow. He picked up his bike and walked it beside her. "This one time we came out in the bush, a bunch of us kids. We saw the northern lights dancing high above us, green and turquoise. And Waawaate starts whistling. All the kids got scared and yelled at him: 'No,' 'Don't,' 'You're not supposed to do that!' And we're freaking out, but you know how he is . . . he has that big grin on his face, and he keeps whistling." Bugz shook her head, smiling. "Then, no word of a lie, the northern lights start getting brighter and brighter. Our eyes must have been as big as cartoon characters'. So Waawaate starts hamming it up—he dances around and starts whistling a song. And I kid you not, the northern lights start getting even brighter and they even change color." Bugz chuckled silently. "They turned all shades of pink, and they're so bright, you wouldn't believe it. I swear to god, they were getting closer to us too. Finally, Waawaate finishes his song, and it breaks the spell. One of the kids runs away, and then we all start running away, running for our lives. Waawaate's chasing after us, yelling through the bush, 'Waawaate niin! Waawaate niin!!'—which means 'I am the northern lights!'" Bugz was still smiling. "Anyways, I hated him for about two days straight after that for scaring me. But now . . ."

"What a great memory." Feng smiled too. He looked to the sky and back to Bugz. "First time I saw the northern lights was on a postcard Liumei sent me from Alaska. I thought they were magic. They were in the shape of the infinity symbol. She wrote about how it reminded her of home. The infinity symbol means good luck to us."

"Here, it's the symbol of the Métis."

"What?" Feng asked.

"Métis. The people of the Red River. They're the descendants of the Anishinaabe and Cree who married the French and Scottish fur traders."

"Really?"

"Yup. They've got their own language, Michif. Their own culture. They even have their own flag. It's got a giant infinity symbol on it."

"Cool."

"Yeah, it is. The two sides of their heritage, united. Forever."

Feng leaned his bike on a tree and used a stick to trace an infinity symbol in the earth in front of them. "Look what I made you."

Bugz grinned. "Wherever did you get the idea for that symbol?"

"It represents our two sides, me and you, coming together," Feng said, doing everything he could to not laugh.

"Yech." Bugz pretended to gag. "Don't disrespect the great Métis nation with your cheesy pick-up lines."

She laughed and waved Feng away. As he chuckled, she took a fork in the path away from the spot they'd visited before. They headed deeper into the forest.

CHAPTER 38

Bugz led Feng through a cedar bog and into a clearing. At its center stood a huge circle formed by large rocks stacked on top of one another.

"Here it is," Bugz announced, walking up to the oracle. "The Thunderbird's Nest."

"I can't even see anything," Feng said, enraptured by the autumnal glow of his phone. "It's nothing but energy."

"Put your phone away. You're going to let your stupid friends know where we are."

"Right." Feng complied. "So this is your secret."

"This is my secret."

Bugz sat down on the earth beside the nest and patted a spot beside her. Feng sat, legs crossed. He watched as Bugz closed her eyes and whispered a prayer in the Anishinaabe language beneath her breath. When she opened her eyes Feng quickly cast his gaze away, as though he'd been staring at something else.

"I don't know why you're nervous." Bugz broke the silence. "I always feel at peace when I come here. It's the only time I feel this calm. In the real world, anyway."

"What is this place, really?"

"I told you—it's a Thunderbird's Nest," she said seriously, before cracking a smile. "My dad brought us here when we were kids. We'd come here and make a tobacco offering before we'd go hunting or picking medicine in the area."

Bugz pulled a curved blade with a wooden handle from her pocket. It looked more like a carving knife than a weapon.

"He gave me this on one of those trips." She handed it to Feng. "I bring it with me everywhere I go." He nodded and handed it back before motioning to the nest.

"Who built it?"

"Thunderbirds, obviously."

"I'm guessing a Thunderbird is one of those giant eagles with the lightning bolts that you ride around on in the 'Verse."

"Yup."

"But who built this one in the real world?"

"Thunderbirds did." Bugz appeared to study the lichen growing on the rocks closest to her. "That's my story and I'm sticking with it."

"I don't believe that," Feng said.

"Believe it," Bugz replied.

"Seriously, though, what is this place?" he asked.

"This is where the Thunderbirds are born. My Ancestors came here to thank them for taking care of us, for bringing the storms that nourish the land in the summer and scaring off the underwater panthers that threaten us."

"I thought that leopard-snake thing was your friend."

"He is. But my Ancestors were afraid of his kind." Bugz turned to face a puzzled Feng. "Hey, sometimes you've got to be bad if you wanna be this good."

Feng laughed at her unexpected swagger, apparently unsure if his automatic translator was working properly.

"Anyway, if you're asking why this place made me so good in the Floraverse, I don't know," Bugz said. "Call it a glitch, call it the nexus between the real world and the digital world. Whatever it is, when I come here to do something in the 'Verse, it supercharges it."

Feng spun his phone in his hand, listening intently. He spun the phone again before bringing it to rest under his chin. "Still, you have some pretty crazy reflexes," he added. "I bet anyone could come here and they still wouldn't understand the 'Verse the way you do."

"This is only half of my secret." Bugz looked off into the distance beyond the nest. "There's another stone formation like this in the Spirit World, at the bottom of Lake of the Torches. We found it when Mishi-pizhiw and the Thunderbirds were tearing up the land. A stone ring buried deep underground. Now it's Mishi-pizhiw's nest."

"So you can supercharge stuff there too."

Bugz nodded. "It's more than that," she said, preparing herself for his reaction to what she was about to reveal. She inhaled. "It's a respawn point into the Spirit World."

"That's not possible. You have to respawn in AR first and work your way back to the Spirit World."

Bugz shook her head. "Put your headset on and go to Mishi-pizhiw's nest. It's at the bottom of the lake."

Feng quickly followed her instructions. "Okay, now what?" Feng asked from behind his headset, his 'Versona swimming around on-screen near the periphery of Mishi-pizhiw's nest.

"Destroy my 'Versona," Bugz said.

"No. It'll take you forever to get back."

"Just do it."

"No. I don't believe you."

"Fine." Bugz put her headset on. After a few blinks, her 'Versona slumped to the seafloor in the Spirit World and her gamertag rose slowly. Feng's jaw dropped.

In the real world, Bugz lifted her headset and walked to the center of the nest, phone in hand and AR mode activated. As she reached the middle of the real-world nest, her 'Versona suddenly reappeared in front of Feng in the center of Mishi-pizhiw's nest in the Spirit World, sparkling and shimmering with energy. Her experience points, bitcoins, and gifts returned at their previous level. Her 'Versona, operating under AI, stepped out of the digital nest in the Spirit World completely rejuvenated.

Feng removed his headset and re-engaged with Bugz in the real world. His eyes widened. "No wonder you're so much better!" He shook his head in disbelief. "While everyone else wastes their time clawing their way back to the Spirit World, you can just dive right back in."

Bugz felt a pang. Feng's reaction was just what she'd feared. She'd rushed to tell him because she wanted to trust him completely. To dismiss whatever remained of her concerns about him. A part of her had secretly hoped he'd hear the news and tell her it didn't matter because he—and only he—saw the innate talent deep inside her that accounted for her greatness.

"You kept experimenting, going big and failing, all the while building your skills because you knew even if you died, you'd just respawn. Meanwhile, the rest of us waited months, even years, to get a chance to try again." Feng spoke for his own benefit, seeming oblivious to Bugz's presence now.

"Okay." Bugz felt as if the blood beneath her skin was growing hotter and hotter. *You don't know how hard I've worked at this.* A wave of stress coursed through her body.

"Wow, I wish I could've had this . . ."

"Why? So you could've joined Clan:LESS quicker?" Bugz took a deep breath.

"If I had this, I wouldn't need a clan. I'd be solo, just like you."

"You could never do what I do." Bugz stood and turned to leave. "I shouldn't've told you."

Feng looked at her, puzzled. "I'm sorry." He appeared unsure what to say next, but took a step forward. "Don't leave." He reached for her hand, and Bugz let him take it. "I'm glad you told me."

Bugz nodded. She felt the warmth of Feng's palm enveloping her fingers. She wondered if her hands felt sweaty. "You know what's messed up? The nest really is a sacred site. It's been important to my people for millennia." She scanned their surroundings. "But what gave it power in the Floraverse is that it's a glitch. Some problem with the map. It screws phones up when they come here." She tilted her head skyward. She and Feng held hands as they looked at the twinkling stars above. A meteor streaked across the sky.

"Ursa Major." Feng named the constellation the shooting star cut across.

"Binesi." Bugz called it by its Anishinaabe name, the word for Thunderbird. They stood for a while, watching the silent sky above.

"How do you like that? A glitch in the map." Bugz turned to face Feng, who met her gaze. "They've mapped everything in the world—the deep seas, even parts of space. They've mapped it all perfectly. Everything except the Rez. They never thought to map the Rez." Bugz laughed. "But I took that glitch and did something with it. I turned it into my superpower." She cocked her head. "It's kind of like what we did with the Rez itself. They gave us scraps and we made it food."

A bat flew by just over their heads. "No one knows I still come here. Not even my dad. I think everyone's forgotten about this place except me."

A firefly lit up and danced in the air above them.

"So . . ." Bugz smiled and took a half step closer to Feng. "Can you keep my secret?"

"Absolutely."

CHAPTER 39

Bugz couldn't escape the eerie dream. Unlike in the Floraverse, she couldn't disconnect. She could only step forward.

Bugz was a child again, carried in her mother's arms. They stood in a Sundance arbor, the site of that most sacred of ceremonies, as her father prepared to pierce. Bugz recognized the scene as one of her childhood memories—an old sepia filmstrip, everything soaked in a warm honey glow. She saw her father's chapped lips. He'd fasted, without food or water, for four days as part of the ceremony. Frank shuffled slowly, tired from dancing since before dawn on each of those days.

Bugz watched her father step forward onto a buffalo robe and pop two small black wooden pegs in his mouth. A Sundancer grabbed her father's upper arm, pinching the skin between his fingers and lancing it with a scalpel.

The dancer pushed the blade through until it emerged from Frank's skin a half-inch away. A second dancer slid one of the wooden pegs through the hole. The two men repeated the process on the other arm; then they shook hands and hugged her dad. He turned to face Bugz. She could only focus on the wooden peg embedded in each of his arms. Summer and Bugz followed Frank to a spot farther away in the arbor, where he retrieved a forked rope tied to the tree at the center of the space. The Sundancers harnessed each end of the rope to the pegs in her father's arms.

Bugz watched from the safety of her mother's embrace as her father danced in place and stared at the tree, blood slowly trickling from his arms. Summer blew the eagle whistle she wore around her neck. After a small eternity, Frank ran backward until the tightening rope ripped the pegs from his skin and sent the harness flying back toward the tree.

"Why did Daddy do that?" Bugz asked her mother.

"Because he wants his prayers to come true."

"But why not just give tobacco?"

"Because the Creator made everything. Sacrificing a piece of ourselves is the only thing we can really *give* to the Creator," her mom explained, wiping away a tear.

Summer put Bugz down on the ground and suddenly the skies clouded over. Everything turned cold, dark, and gray. The leaves fell from the cottonwood tree; only the dry, dead branches remained, clawing the sky. Bugz looked down at her arms and saw she was marked for the piercing ceremony. She'd never pierced before. Now she knew her dream was drifting from memory and taking her someplace new. Her heart raced.

Bugz saw Waawaate walking to her with a scalpel in his hand. She knew he would cut her, even if the look on his face said he didn't want to. He touched the skin on her shoulder.

Bugz woke up with a start. Scanning her darkened room, she fumbled for her phone and found its reassuring glow.

CHAPTER 40

The bullets screamed down, their tracers illuminating the darkness around Lake of the Torches. Artillery crashed through rain onto the pebble beach, pinning Bugz down behind two large boulders. She stuck one eye out around the corner and pulled back instantly. A barrage of laser fire exploded on the spot where her head had been. Bugz couldn't find any room to maneuver. Clan:LESS had caught her completely off guard this time.

Why didn't I see them coming?

A helicopter gunship dropped from the sky just a few dozen yards away from Bugz, cutting her self-interrogation short. The ship opened fire. Bugz dove into a ninja roll to escape the bullets, which riddled the ground behind her. She ran along the shore, away from the horde, knowing they'd pounce on her again in an instant. She waved her hand and giant roots shot up from the nearby forest floor, but the upgraded Clan:LESS weapons tore them to shreds faster than they had in the past. Nothing Bugz did bought her enough time.

Alpha jumped from the helicopter and landed on the shores of the lake in a kneeling position. As he stood slowly, somehow taller than before, Bugz tried for a second time to summon the plant life. But this time, Alpha anticipated the maneuver and fired napalm across the forest canopy, which disintegrated on impact. Birds scattered into the sky, melting to the ground while still attempting flight. They fell like a dark and disturbing rain. Animals scurried and ran for their lives but most moved too slowly. Alpha kept firing on the forest creatures and they burned alive. They roared and bit at their own backs and hind legs in futile attempts to stop the damage.

Bugz howled.

Mishi-pizhiw roared from the depths of Lake of the Torches with demon-red eyes aglow, contrasting brilliantly against the torrential downpour and the darkness around him. He spewed a stream of fire down on the Clan:LESS horde. But they matched him move for move. They raised clear Gorilla Glass shields and hunkered down to wait out the attack. Alpha ran to his troops and slid down under the shields.

"Assemble the gun!" he yelled over the voice-com as he planted his energy cannon firmly into the sand beside him.

Soldiers scrambled around him, some raising shields to protect their workspace. They affixed five additional energy cannons to the first in a shape reminiscent of a revolver's chambers, and connected other pieces of machinery and stabilizing structures. They quickly built a huge rapid-fire cannon.

Two dozen more helicopter gunships descended from the clouds. They encircled Mishi-pizhiw and opened fire, concentrating their barrage on the horned serpent's head. He banked from side to side, trying to dodge their guns, but with the ships raining bullets down from every direction, he could do nothing but plunge back into the waters.

Bugz used the momentary distraction to duck back behind the boulders. She closed her eyes and summoned backup. Soon, the lake rippled with waves as a phalanx of diamondback sturgeon sped quickly to the shore. The first three of these humongous bottom-feeders plowed into the closest Clan:LESS soldiers. Shield or not, the impact was deadly. Gamertags rose to the heavens.

Another wave of sturgeon attacked, but this time the massive mega–Gatling gun was operational. It whirred to life and pitched a rapid, repeating stream of energy bolts directly at the sturgeon bearing down on the Clan:LESS warriors, destroying the gigantic fish.

The skies opened, revealing a new moon and starry night. From this hole in the sky, a fleet of twenty Thunderbirds descended. They screamed as they dive-bombed the helicopter gunships. With the element of surprise on her side, the lead Thunderbird sent one chopper spiraling down to the earth with several well-timed thunderbolts. The aircraft exploded on impact. The gamertags of all those aboard escaped the wreckage. The remaining helicopters regrouped and launched a counteroffensive against the birds. They succeeded in knocking two birds from the sky, evening the odds slightly. Another Thunderbird broke from the pack and swooped down to retrieve Bugz from her hiding place.

With shoulders slumped, Bugz slunk away from the fighting. She knew the horde had found the nest under Lake of the Torches without her noticing. Bugz could feel the balance of power across the 'Verse shifting away from her.

CHAPTER 41

The Thunderbird carried Bugz in a long looping arc over the lake waters before swinging back toward the battle. As she did, the immense carnage of the scene below came into view.

Dozens of sturgeon floated in the water, each white belly turned to the sky announcing the defeat of an underwater dinosaur. Bugz thought of each one, the time she'd spent creating them; now they'd died without attention or ceremony.

Above this scene of decimation, a desperate dogfight raged in the sky. The Thunderbirds were engaged in an all-out battle with the helicopter corps. Bugz yelled at the Thunderbirds to focus on one helicopter. She held on to the back of her bird's neck with a death grip as the thunder-being fired several bolts at the target. Another Thunderbird turned and fired at the same chopper. The combined lightning fire overwhelmed the helicopter's evasive maneuvers, and it exploded into a shower of flames, pieces of the wreckage crashing into the shallows. The explosion attracted the attention of the horde.

"Get them!" Alpha shouted. He pointed to the sky.

His soldiers obliged, opening fire on the Thunderbirds. Rapid pulses of energy tore through one and sent her in a death spiral toward the lake. She crashed into the waves and sank below. The Clan:LESS gunners took down another and another. For a second, the tableau of the battle showed eight massive and beautiful Thunderbirds falling, their black-and-blue eagle-shaped bodies careening out of control as gunfire and laser beams crisscrossed their doomed trajectories. They crashed to the earth with finality. The way of life that Bugz had recreated in the 'Verse was disappearing before her eyes.

As the horde shot at the last of the Thunderbirds, one flew close to the bird carrying Bugz and glided next to them in silence for a moment. The Thunderbird smiled at Bugz, a pure smile, eyes given over to it. Bugz shook her head.

The smiling Thunderbird banked away and descended on a kamikaze mission to take out the mega–Gatling gun. Another Thunderbird recognized the plan and followed suit. As the birds approached their destinies, their bodies were lit up with energy fire. The Thunderbirds were terminated while still in the air, but momentum carried their bodies forward, crashing them into the mega–Gatling gun and shattering it to pieces. The impact threw the gunners and Alpha backward. The Thunderbirds' sacrifice gave the lone surviving bird, carrying Bugz, a chance to escape. Still, the helicopters closed in.

CHAPTER 42

Feng finally logged into the Floraverse, his aunt having filled the earlier part of his day with chores. The eyes of Feng's 'Versona, run by his bot up until this point, twinkled with a higher degree of awareness as they came under Feng's control. From his post amid his clanmates, Feng scanned the battlefield: dozens of expired sturgeon in the water, Thunderbirds piled on the shore, a burning forest, animal skeletons all around, scores of bodies of former Clan:LESS soldiers. Smoke rose from the rubble. As he turned, he could make out Bugz's figure on the back of the Thunderbird the gunships chased. They fired repeatedly and did immense damage to the bird's wings. The Thunderbird finally crashed to the earth and sent Bugz sprawling to the ground. She slid face-first through the sand.

Mishi-pizhiw rose again from the lake and snapped at the gunships. They dodged him once or twice, but with the mega–Gatling gun now out of commission, the creature had the upper hand. He snatched the first chopper like a cat grabbing a bird. Mishi-pizhiw tossed the crumpled mess at the horde and gamertags popped out of the wreckage. He made short work of the remaining helicopters as well, but a new group of gunners moved into position, reassembled the mega–Gatling gun and targeted him.

"Fire!" Alpha shouted.

They unloaded the gun on Mishi-pizhiw and he dove back into the waters.

"The girl!" Alpha shouted again.

Bugz lay still in the sand. Feng couldn't tell if she'd been knocked out or had simply quit. The gunners took aim at her motionless figure. Adrenaline roared through Feng's body. As the gun glowed, preparing to fire, Feng broke rank. He turned and ran toward the gunners, shoulder-checking them as hard as he could. A few stumbled to the ground, dislodging the gun from its support structure in the process. It fired randomly into the sky.

"Traitor!" Alpha pulled a laser gun and fired at Feng, who now sprinted away down the beach.

The entire Clan:LESS horde gave chase.

Mishi-pizhiw jumped from the lake and assumed his land form. He picked Feng up by his neck like a puppy and tossed him onto his own back. The giant panther sprinted down the beach toward Bugz, who stirred to life and hopped back on the Thunderbird. But the Thunderbird was near death. She jumped into the air only to stumble back to the beach. She couldn't take flight. Time and time again she leapt, but never found lift—and the enemy was closing in. Mishi-pizhiw quickly overtook the Thunderbird and tossed both the bird and Bugz onto his back. The panther made three giant leaps, leaving massive pawprints in the beach as he went, and ran for the hills.

The Clan:LESS horde broke off their pursuit, though Feng could still hear them cursing him over voice-com and see Alpha's livestream in his heads-up display. He watched as Alpha ordered all the Clan:LESS boats to assemble in the center of Lake of the Torches. Once the flotilla gathered, he regaled his crew with tales of their victory.

"Best part is, she won't be coming back anytime soon," Alpha shouted. "Not only did we find her power source, but, after today's battle, it's ours. We control the most powerful resource in the 'Verse! We must always win!"

His troops roared in approval. Feng cut the feed.

Miles away, on the back of a still sprinting Mishi-pizhiw, Feng smoothed the feathers of the catastrophically injured Thunderbird. Bugz looked on with tears in her eyes. Of all of Bugz's creations, Feng realized, the bird and the cat were all that remained. He didn't have much left either, not after deserting his clan.

They fled through the 'Verse, alone, with only each other.

CHAPTER 43

With a moan, Waawaate turned to face Bugz, who sat in a chair next to his hospital bed. A heart monitor beeped. An IV dripped. A fan on one of the electrical components whirred dimly in the background. His illness seemed to be progressing rapidly, and Bugz could read the signs on his face. Chapped lips, pale skin. He smiled. As weak as he looked, his eyes still twinkled. He'd gone home a few days after his collapse and diagnosis, but returned to the hospital after passing out again. The internet's most dire predictions about his condition ran through Bugz's head over and over again.

"Hey." Bugz made note of Waawaate's raspy voice as he spoke. "Do you think you could get me a pop from the vending machine downstairs?"

"Umm, are you allowed to have that?" Bugz asked.

"It's not going to kill me."

"Don't talk like that."

"I never knew you to be superstitious, Bugz. Well, get me a diet pop then. Seriously, diabetes is the least of my worries right now."

"Waawaate, I was watching videos on cancer, and you have to eat right too . . ."

"I will. I just want a pop, okay? I'll get right back to the straight and narrow after." Waawaate grinned, flashing Bugz a glimpse of his charm. She relented with a nod and left to fill his order, scanning her phone the entire time. She bumped into Feng and together they carried two sodas to Waawaate's room.

Pushing the door open, Bugz froze momentarily when she saw the visitors. Stormy, seated on the end of Waawaate's bed, turned and flashed Bugz a huge smile. Chalice sat in the chair Bugz had occupied a few minutes ago.

"Hey, Bugz!" Stormy beamed, all of her perfect white teeth visible. "I figured we'd see you here. I'm really sorry for how things went down last time. Really sorry."

Waawaate looked on with a faint smile.

"Me too, Bugz." Chalice cleared her throat. "That wasn't the real me. I get carried away sometimes, and I'm sorry for what I said to you. You too, Feng."

"Did my brother ask you to say that?" Bugz claimed the chair on the far side of the hospital bed. Feng chose to remain standing. She handed a soda to Waawaate, who handed it back and nodded for her to open it. The bottle made the sound of an eager release.

"No, I didn't ask them," Waawaate said after taking a sip of his drink. "But I'm glad they did. Thanks, girls."

"Alright, well, thanks then," Bugz said nervously. She held her phone up to examine her reflection and fiddled with her hair quickly. Nonchalantly, she checked the appearance of the other two young women in the Floraverse. They'd upgraded. But they'd bought their new skins from influencers again. Some boys might like them, but a real gamer would give them no cred for using those. She glanced at Feng. His expression was serious.

"Just with everything going on, with our hero here down but not out"—Stormy smiled at Waawaate—"it really puts things into perspective. I hope we can be friends again."

"Friends?" Bugz felt lighter for hearing Stormy describe their relationship as such. She'd always assumed any conversation between them was only a transaction. *My friend Stormy.* Bugz tried the phrase on in her head.

"Let's be friends!" Chalice said with forced exuberance. The young women and Waawaate laughed. Feng looked on skeptically. Stormy pulled out her phone and smiled as she saw Bugz's 'Versona through her screen. She turned to Chalice and they looked at each other through their own devices.

"Damn girl," Stormy exclaimed. "Twinsies!"

"Twinning is winning!" Chalice fired back.

Bugz's mom and dad walked in with Liumei and exchanged pleasantries with the visitors. They asked about Stormy's parents, grandparents, and second cousins, as is the Anishinaabe custom. She assured them of everyone's health. They asked Chalice who her mom and dad were again, as is the Anishinaabe custom with people less familiar to you. They nodded, and a few seconds later explained how they all formed an extended family. "So I guess that makes you and Bugz cousins," Bugz's father concluded. "How do you like that, Chalice?" Chalice flashed an uncomfortable smile.

"That means you and Waawaate are cousins, girl!" Stormy said with a huge grin. "So hands off!" The room laughed. "Omigod, I'm so sorry, Mr. and Mrs. Holiday. I don't know why I said that. I'm totally not like that!" Stormy flashed a mischievous glance at Waawaate.

After a few no-kissing-cousins jokes, the room settled down. Frank and Summer became serious. "Excuse us, kids. Can we take some time alone with Waawaate?" Summer asked. "We need to discuss a few things."

"Sure, can we come back up later?" Stormy asked, and received a nod from Summer. "Alright then, maybe we'll just go wait downstairs." She led Chalice out of the room.

Bugz looked to her parents and found silence. They wanted her to leave too. She glanced at Feng and he followed her out of the room.

CHAPTER 44

As Bugz and Feng waited for the elevator, he looked at her and shook his head. "Bugz, those girls are fake."

"We're all fake." Bugz showed him a screen cap of her 'Versona.

"Not like them. Be careful . . ." The sliding elevator doors interrupted him, opening to reveal Stormy and Chalice. They broke out giggling.

"We must be lost," Chalice said.

"No problem, we'll show you out," Feng said.

Chalice and Stormy exchanged glances. Bugz buried her face in her phone. From the elevator, they walked out to the front steps and onto the asphalt loop the ambulances used to access the hospital's ER. The warm air of the summer evening felt good on Bugz's skin. The two girls traded pulls from a vape pen and blew the smoke high into the air above them.

"Mine's better, I look like a dragon," Stormy said of her cloud, smiling.

"You look like a dinosaur," Chalice teased.

"Is that an 'old' joke? The reason I'm a grade ahead of you is cause you failed, missy. We are the same age!"

"I didn't fail . . . I just didn't get all the credits I should've."

Stormy laughed.

Feng crossed the street and sat on a nearby picnic table. Bugz followed him; Stormy and Chalice too. Feng immediately dove into the Floraverse and swiped through updates. Bugz grimaced as she did the same. Chalice pulled out her phone and scrolled through her messages.

"Oh shoot, I forgot my phone," Stormy said. "Must be upstairs." She led Chalice back into the hospital.

"Things are getting pretty bad for us in the 'Verse," Bugz said. "I can't turn this thing around without Mishi-pizhiw's nest." Bugz noticed a scowl on Feng's face. "What's up?"

"Nothing."

"Come on, obviously something's bothering you."

"I'm just reading through my messages. And they're nothing but hate mail from all my clanmates." Feng swiped quickly through the feed. "*Former* clanmates, I guess." He shook his head. "They all think I'm a traitor. Some are even talking about doxing me. Here, look."

As Feng's fingers swiped through his inbox, Bugz scanned a series of insults, memes, and outright hate speech, all of it way too familiar to her.

"That's really bad." Bugz thought of biting her tongue but decided not to. "But you know what? That's exactly the type of thing your friends do to me. Just be glad they didn't make any deep fakes of you."

Feng scrunched up his nose.

"I told you. Neo-alt-right losers."

"They're still my bros."

"What? Look at that one right there. That's racist." Bugz pointed out a particularly offensive meme Feng had received.

"Well, some of them haven't done anything. Like the ones I'm really close with. Behemoth, Joe . . ." Feng seemed to search for a third name to add to his list.

"But they're not stopping it either, are they?" Bugz said quietly, sensing that she'd pushed Feng toward his limit.

"Those guys got my back." Feng continued shaking his head as his lips pursed tightly. "*Had* my back."

Bugz nodded. "I know what you're going through. I've been there. You feel a knot in the pit of your stomach, knowing that people are talking about you. You want to reply to every single message, don't you? Argue every single point?"

"Yeah . . ."

"But you also know it's pointless, right? There's no argument you can make that will win a meme war."

"I guess."

"Anyway, all I'm saying is I hope maybe now you realize the truth about your friends."

Feng looked away.

"The Floraverse is so cool. But people like Clan:LESS prevent others from enjoying it."

Feng finally re-engaged. "Sure, whatever. But you don't know what it was like for me. When it was tough for me as a kid at school, who was there for me? My parents? Liumei? You? No, none of you were there. Clan:LESS was." Feng's jaw tightened visibly. "Alpha was there for me. First, just as someone to look up to on streams. And then he actually reached out and invited me in. You know what it means to have someone you watch stream invite you to play with them?" Feng shook his head. "I could always talk to the guys in Clan:LESS and go on missions with them, no matter what was happening in the rest of my life." He sniffed hard and wiped his nose. "And now it's over."

Bugz nodded.

"I don't even know if it was worth it."

Bugz stopped nodding.

Stormy and Chalice walked back across the paved road playing on their phones. They took their seats on the picnic table again. Stormy eyed Bugz and Feng.

"What'd we interrupt? You two love birds having a lovers' quarrel?" Chalice giggled.

"Shut up," Bugz said with a smile. She glanced at Feng and, seeing him downcast, set her face into a more serious expression. "What were they doing when you went in?"

"Still talking," Stormy replied.

"His aunt was there too," Chalice added, nodding to Feng.

"Sounded like some pretty serious stuff," Stormy added.

"Life and death."

CHAPTER 45

Bugz stroked the feathers above the Thunderbird's eye. The bird sat on a rock face above the shores of another lake.

"C'mon now, Binesi!" Bugz called out. The Thunderbird straightened up, and after a few false starts she managed to fly up to a nearby tree branch. The massive cedar swayed under her weight as though caught in a strong wind.

Suddenly, a thick laser beam crashed into the treetop and sent the Thunderbird falling toward the ground.

"Clan:LESS!" Feng pointed to a nearby rock hill. As he shot off the first few rounds from his machine gun, a small horde of Clan:LESS mercenaries crested the hilltop and returned fire.

"Mishi-pizhiw, help!" Bugz shouted to the nearby lake. The beast emerged instantly from the water and she jumped onto its back. Bugz wanted to fight, but her

Thunderbird couldn't withstand much more damage. "C'mon, Binesi! Feng! Let's go!" she shouted. The Thunderbird, suddenly charged with virtual adrenaline, jumped into the air and caught a flight path that mirrored the underwater panther's trajectory on the water's surface. Feng jumped from the shore and climbed aboard Mishi-pizhiw's back. Bugz fired over Feng's head, with guns in both hands, at the growing horde gathering on the shore they'd just left behind.

Bugz screamed at Mishi-pizhiw to speed up and they disappeared around an island, leaving the clan out of sight. She cried for the supernatural creature to go faster. After catching her breath, and after darting around a few more islands, Bugz assumed they'd covered enough distance to find some reprieve.

She noticed motion from the corner of her eye on their starboard side. She turned and saw a fleet of Clan:LESS helicopters closing in on them. *How did they find us?* she wondered. Bugz jumped into the air and fired off several rounds at two of the choppers, aiming for the pilots. The aircraft spun toward the lake and crashed to the surface.

Mishi-pizhiw turned and struck at another of the choppers like an attack dog hitting the end of his leash. He captured the helicopter in his jaws and crushed everyone on board, doing away with them instantly.

"Let's dive, in three . . ."

Bugz looked nervously at the Thunderbird hurtling toward her under enemy fire.

"Two . . ."

The bird took fire again. Bugz jumped to helicopter height and dispatched another ship with sniper-like accuracy. The chopper spun toward the lake as Bugz and the Thunderbird both fell toward Mishi-pizhiw.

"One . . ."

As Bugz finished her countdown, Feng fired several rounds at the remaining helicopters with an angry look on his face. Bugz wondered if he really regretted turning on his clan. She landed with a thud beside Feng and gripped Mishi-pizhiw's back. The Thunderbird landed on top of Bugz and Feng, covering them both with her wings, and dug her talons into Mishi-pizhiw. The creature roared.

Bugz yelled, "Dive!"

The beast plowed his head into the water below. They disappeared within a fraction of a second. The helicopters circled their last visible location on the lake's surface, puncturing the waves with random gunfire and searchlights.

CHAPTER 46

Beneath the waves, Mishi-pizhiw dove deeper and deeper into the depths of this lake. His undulating form was like that seen in photos of the Loch Ness monster. He whipped his tail up and down to propel them deeper still. The lake seemed bottomless.

"There's a series of underwater caves we can escape to," Bugz said through her voice-com. Feng nodded before Bugz continued. "Those tunnels lead to another lake far from here, so we should be able to buy some time to regroup." She glanced at the chat screen in her heads-up display.

"KnightSuper: You're doing great girl"

"Monkey97: Here's some coin to help . . ."

"Persephoney: Where are you going?"

"TheRealClanWithout: You're a fraud!!!"

Bugz silenced the chat and killed her livestream. It

only served to distract now. The gifts she received had slowed considerably since Alpha took over Mishi-pizhiw's nest. Clan:LESS had overtaken her as the game's leading players shortly thereafter, and their resources continued to expand rapidly. A school of thought went viral online, arguing Bugz never deserved the stature she'd once enjoyed. Trolls reminded Bugz of this every time she opened a chat window. They'd harass her, taunt her, and otherwise remind her how terrible the online world could be for a young woman. Bugz tried to ignore this online chatter, but the number of followers she'd lost bothered her.

Mishi-pizhiw entered the jaws of a massive cave opening. The entrance looked like a giant underwater demon's mouth agape, set to swallow them whole. Suddenly, they found themselves in total darkness. Bugz squirmed out from under the Thunderbird, climbed up Mishi-pizhiw's back to his head, and gripped his horns. She steered him through the winding cave structures using the night-vision in her heads-up display. They banked sharply to their port side to avoid a massive stalactite, and continued toward a straightaway, passing a school of cavefish heading in the opposite direction.

That's weird. They should be swimming away from us rather than toward us, Bugz thought. *There shouldn't be anything else down here. They should be afraid of us.*

Bugz throttled Mishi-pizhiw's horns forward and they dove into a tunnel that took them several hundred feet deeper before banking sharply to a horizontal plane. Instantly, Bugz's night-vision blazed white-hot and blinded her. Purely by touch, she flipped off the night-vision and saw a bright light ahead of them. The narrow tunnel shaft offered no room in which to turn around.

"Feng, get up here!" she yelled. "How did they find us?!"

Mishi-pizhiw gritted his teeth and picked up speed rapidly, hoping to plow through whatever waited for them at tunnel's end—one hundred feet, fifty feet, twenty-five.

Mishi-pizhiw shot out of the tunnel and found himself surrounded by a fleet of Clan:LESS submarines.

"There's no way they could've known we were down here!" Bugz yelled. "There's no way. Did you message them?!" She shoved Feng's shoulder.

"No!" he yelled back. "I swear. They cut me off voice-com and the group chat."

"Then how did they know?!"

"Don't even start. After everything I'm going through for helping you. Everything I gave up." Feng shook his head in anger.

Bugz gritted her teeth as she unholstered two guns and blasted her weapons at the nearest submarine. A depth charge exploded off her starboard side and sent her careening off Mishi-pizhiw's back. The massive serpent charged a nearby submarine and crushed it in his jaws like a shark tearing through a rowboat. Gamertags floated up from the wreckage. His enemies changed tack.

One sub plowed ahead of Mishi-pizhiw, acting as a

lure, while three broke off and covered his flank. The three subs began firing at the Thunderbird on his back, now completely defenseless underwater. Bugz noticed and shouted. Mishi-pizhiw grabbed hold of the decoy sub and turned to attack the others, but it was too late. Their laser fire loosened the grip of the Thunderbird's talons and she sank down to the cave floor.

The Clan:LESS soldiers continued firing on the bird as Mishi-pizhiw dispatched the subs attacking him one by one. The remains of the submarines crashed into the cave floor not far from the nearly lifeless Thunderbird. The reverberations reached Bugz, who fired at still more submarines from a perch behind a stalagmite. She destroyed all but one with her deadeye shots. Feng exchanged fire with the remaining sub—a nuclear vessel and the largest in the fleet.

Bugz turned to see her beautiful bird crumpled on the floor of the cave. She swam as quickly as she could to the bird's side. Bugz took heavy fire from the remaining sub as it broke away from its gunfight with Feng. Reinforcement subs poured into the cave and quickly engaged Feng and Mishi-pizhiw, bombing them with torpedoes.

Bugz cradled the bird's massive head in her arms. She stroked her beak. The nuclear submarine prepared to fire, but Bugz turned and with three shots took out its weapons systems. Damaged but not destroyed, the hull of the sub began to turn a translucent orange. Inside the vessel, the crew engineered a meltdown, intending to crash into

Bugz while the nuclear core on board exploded with cataclysmic radiation. It was closing in on Bugz fast, but she refused to let go of her Thunderbird.

As the submarine prepared to ram Bugz, the Thunderbird summoned the last of her strength and snatched the sub in her talons. The vessel shook in her claws as the radioactive decay hit a critical point. Bugz kissed the Thunderbird and pushed off the lake bottom. Kicking furiously, she put as much space as she could between herself and the imminent explosion.

Mishi-pizhiw pulled Bugz and Feng into the tunnel with only a fraction of a second to spare. He plugged the mouth of the tunnel with his diamond back and prepared to absorb the energy of the blast.

Daylight engulfed the cave as the nuclear sub exploded, incinerating the submarine instantly, and the Thunderbird along with it. The blast destroyed all of the other Clan:LESS ships as well.

Once the shockwave cleared and the boiling water cooled sufficiently, Mishi-pizhiw returned to the scene of the battle and looked sadly toward the floor of the lake. Bugz swam to the edge of the cave and looked down. She saw the lifeless Thunderbird, the last of her kind, petrified in ash. The bird lay with wings spread like an eagle on a coat of arms, still clutching the wreckage of the nuclear sub in its talons. Bugz bit her bottom lip.

Feng swam past her to assess the scene for himself. "I'm so sorry, Bugz," he said over voice-com.

As Feng swam ahead of Bugz, she saw the back of his neck . . . a glowing orb flashed red. It took a second for Bugz to register what the light meant. She didn't want to believe she'd seen it, or to accept the betrayal the red light represented, but it flashed again just the same. A tracking device. Feng had led them to her. It was all his fault. Her eyes filled with tears. Adrenaline shot to the ends of her nerves. She drew her obsidian sword.

"COWARD!" Bugz screamed. "You did this—you did all of this! And you never even had the courage to face me. You never had the courage to fight!"

"No, Bugz, I didn't—"

Bugz cut Feng off mid-sentence. She decapitated him with a quick swing of her sword.

For a moment, she studied the shocked expression on Feng's face as his head rotated slowly in the water. Bugz noted the Ø symbol still branded onto Feng's arm. She shook her head.

Once a loser, always a loser.

Bugz turned and grabbed hold of Mishi-pizhiw. His powerful tail propelled them forward as they shot into the cave at great speed. Together, the pair hurtled headlong into the darkness.

CHAPTER 47

A young man staggered through the forest on a shadowy overcast night, holding his glowing phone in front of him to illuminate the darkness that surrounded him. He wore a trucker hat pulled low over his eyes, more for reassurance than subterfuge. *No one is going to recognize me this far from civilization,* he thought to himself. He wore the lumberjack plaid shirt and ripped jeans that were the signature of Clan:LESS members in the real world. On each of his biceps lay matching Ø tattoos. This was the Behemoth, who appeared much more unassuming in the real world than his name suggested.

He tripped over a stump and hit the ground as his phone flew through the air ahead of him. *Damn.* He rubbed his throbbing shin until he regained his bearings. He couldn't see anything around him, the forested surroundings completely foreign to a city kid like him. He scanned left and right before noticing the glowing orb of his phone laying against a tree well outside his reach. He tried to shake the feeling that he'd landed in a writhing mass of maggots. He stood and frantically brushed the pine needles from his clothing.

Slowly, deliberately, and with more than a little fear, he walked forward with his arms stretched out in front of him, sliding his feet on the forest floor as though skiing cross-country. He felt a tree in front of him. Nervously, he felt up and down its skinny trunk and navigated himself around it. His feet ran up against a bush. He crouched down to ascertain its exact shape by touch before slowly stepping over it, still half expecting a bottomless pit to swallow him on the other side. His foot touched solid ground and he breathed a sigh of relief. He saw the glowing rectangle directly in front of him and scooped down to pick it up.

The phone's screen shone brilliantly, bathing everything around it in light, the AR function now almost useless. It'd shone like this for his entire half-hour trek through the forest, but he knew he was near his destination now. He lifted his eyes from his phone and looked ahead. There, in front of him, illuminated only by the light of his handheld screen, lay a clearing.

The Behemoth panted. He lunged forward and tried to run, believing his will would carry him to the finish line. He tripped over a large root and flew again, this time sliding face first into the wet earth.

The Behemoth felt a light rain on the back of his head as he inventoried the damage. His throbbing shin hurt pretty badly once again, and his torso and legs were soaked, but he could still breathe. He'd lost his phone a second time. He pulled himself up and blinked a few times before regaining his vision.

And then he saw it.

His phone lay in the mud many steps ahead of him, but something else grabbed his attention. Looming over the top of his screen like an alien obelisk, bathed in the orange glow, lay a giant rock pile arranged in the shape of a circle. The Thunderbird's Nest. The young man ran toward the nest and launched a video chat as soon as he reached his phone. Alpha and the other Clan:LESS leaders answered the call. The rain picked up as the connection locked in.

"What?" Alpha asked.

"I found it!" the Behemoth yelled, the wind picking up all around him. "I found it! It's just like in the 'Verse—a giant stone circle!"

"You found it?" Alpha asked.

"Yes!"

"Okay." Alpha nodded. "Send us your location. This is excellent. There's no way Bugz can stop us now. Good job, soldier!"

Alpha terminated the call and left the Behemoth sitting alone in the darkness. Rain poured down on his head.

CHAPTER 48

"Bugz, hold up."

She could see Feng approaching in the hallway. Teenagers crowded the space, rushing out of their homerooms. Taking note of the impending confrontation, one passerby tapped a friend and they both stopped to watch.

"I don't want to talk to you," Bugz said, looking at the floor.

"C'mon."

"No."

"Bugz, talk to me!"

"Leave me alone!"

"You owe me an explanation."

At this, Bugz turned and faced Feng with amazement in her eyes. "I owe *you* an explanation?" She amped up her tone. "I don't owe you anything. You destroyed everything I cared about!" Bugz squared up to Feng, clearly challenging him. In spite of her shorter stature, she brought her face to within inches of his.

"What I did to you?" Feng's face contorted in anger. "You eliminated me from the Spirit World! I have to start over from scratch! Do you know how long it took me last time?"

A crowd had gathered in a circle around them now. Every student had seen a stream or a replay of what happened in the Floraverse the night before. They'd all watched Bugz destroy the boy they assumed she loved. Dozens of phones now livestreamed this real-life rematch. The devices' transparent screens revealed the shocked and excited expressions of their users.

"You deserved it," Bugz said. "You brought them to me, and they took everything I had. Everything I gave life to is dead. Everything I did for my culture, it's over. There's only one of my creations left."

"I didn't do anything wrong. I was only trying to help you."

Bugz fought back the urge to scream. She felt like hurting him. She also felt gross for still caring for someone who clearly didn't understand her. Again, she thought of the scars she'd seen on her cousin Ally's arm. A tear escaped down her cheek.

"Oh, she's crying!" A bystander stated the obvious.

"Shut up!" Bugz yelled back. The bystander looked more closely at his phone, as though it would protect him.

"I understand." Feng spoke again. "In the Floraverse,

you *were* brave, but in the real world, you're nothing. Now that you can't magically respawn, that's all you are—nothing."

Bugz brought her sleeve to her face to wipe her eyes. She sniffed and composed herself. She saw through Feng now; his pedestrian insult had somehow calmed her. "I'm sorry I brought you into my life," she said softly. "Everything fell apart once you came along." She studied his irises for a sign of compassion, for a glimpse of humanity, for something. Her search came up empty. "I thought you saw me for who I really am."

"What about me? All the abuse I've been putting up with for you. Now I've got to restart from scratch. And worse yet, no clan is going to want me now that I've been blacklisted by Clan:LESS."

"Who cares? They're a bunch of losers."

"I gave up everything for Clan:LESS. I left my friggin' country for them. And then what did I do? I betrayed them to help you. What a mistake. I'm the one who lost everything!"

"There's a million goons out there like you. You can just buy back every dumb gun and skin you lost." Bugz shook her head. "I can't do that. An entire way of life. A back-up of our civilization. It's over."

"You can respawn!" Feng stretched his arms out as though egging Bugz on to fight him. "Build it again!"

"Feng, just leave."

"No, you have to talk to me! You owe me that."

Bugz turned away. "Just leave," she said, her voice low.

"Fine, I'll leave and go look at some more memes about what a traitor I am. And you can put your fake face and fake body back on and go hide behind your 'Versona." Feng stormed off for a few steps, stopped, and turned. The chatter in the crowd died. Feng stared at Bugz, letting his gaze travel from her head to her toes. "I can't stand how you look without my phone anyway."

CHAPTER 49

Bugz processed the words with detachment as Feng disappeared further into the crowd. The crowd itself seemed to shift nervously, trading shocked expressions. Bugz felt as if she were buried under an avalanche of eyes studying her. She knew if she took her phone out now it would make her seem small and sad, and the action would be immortalized forever on the livestreams. So she chose something slightly more reasonable: she ran. She pushed through the crowd to a nearby accessible restroom and locked the door behind her. She sat in the tiled corner and, letting the tears flow, pulled out her phone and fumbled with it aimlessly.

Bugz heard a knock at the door.

"Go away!" she shouted.

Three more knocks.

"I said, GO AWAY!"

After a pause, a feminine voice snuck through the door. "It's me, Stormy." Stormy waited another moment and spoke again, gently but firmly. "Open up." She rapped softly on the door one final time before Bugz stood and opened it a crack. She knew Stormy could see her red, swollen eyes, but she didn't care.

"Can I come in?" the girl asked.

"I'm not going to hurt myself."

"Well, that's good." Stormy smiled. "But I actually just wanted to ask how you're feeling."

Bugz stepped back from the door and Stormy slid through the opening. Bugz noted Stormy's skinniness.

"That was harsh, bro," Stormy said. "That's why I hate guys our age . . . so immature. Like, you're arguing and they just bring up random stuff to make you feel bad?"

"Yeah . . . ," Bugz responded. She turned and stared into the mirror above the sink. She fiddled with her hair before running the water, splashing it on her face, and checking herself again. She looked like a mess.

"He went crazy on you." Stormy paused for a second and smiled. "Chalice was all 'I told you so!'" Stormy's laugh filled the room. "I'm sorry, but it was funny. Anyway, don't let it get you down. He's not thinking straight. I mean, how could he? Your brother's in the hospital, and he pulls this?"

Bugz nodded. Stormy stood behind her and smiled into the mirror. "Here, let me." She took over from Bugz's fiddling and started pulling Bugz's hair into tight French

222

braids. "Yeah, he went off on you. He must be really mad. Who knew games were so important?"

"It's more than just a game," Bugz said emphatically. She searched Stormy's eyes for understanding.

"It's the money, right?"

"No. I still have everything I saved up." Bugz paused. "You don't understand. It's not just a game. It's my life."

Stormy scrunched her forehead.

The wounded girl continued, "All the time I spent building myself up in the game, everything I created, everything I cared for in there—that's the part you don't understand."

"No, I do understand," Stormy said, still deep in concentration over Bugz's hair. She wet her finger under the faucet and corralled a few stray wisps along Bugz's hairline. "I lost my beadwork in a fire two years ago. All of my fancy shawl regalia, actually." She shook her head and went on. "But it was the beadwork that really got to me. I cried so hard!" Stormy smiled again. "Girl, I cried so hard I'd make your little meltdown here look like a pregame show!"

Bugz grinned.

Stormy picked up her train of thought again. "But yeah, losing that beadwork was really tough. It was like losing my first love or something." Stormy focused intently on shaping Bugz's braids perfectly. "No, really. That was the first set I beaded myself. I poured my heart into it. I worked on it all winter, and then I danced in it all summer, for two summers actually, and then, boom, it was gone."

Bugz thought of Waawaate. She swallowed.

"My kookom taught me how to bead. She used to tell me, 'Say a prayer with every bead you use.'" Stormy did her best grandma impression, even crouching and squinting slightly. "Kookom used to say, 'Your beadwork is a sign of how much you are loved because someone took the time to sew every single bead, and to do it with a prayer, all for you.' So I guess someone really must love you if you got beadwork, right? That's why I bawled like crazy when it burned up, because of all the love that beadwork represented, and losing it meant I lost that love." Stormy sighed. "My first love."

Bugz cried again, though for another reason now. Bugz thought of her relationship with Waawaate as beadwork. Each moment they spent together was a cut-glass bead stitched into the pattern of their lives. Every tear they'd shed together was another contour in a beautiful floral design. Every time she'd watched him working his magic on the pow-wow trail, at the traditional ceremonies, making people laugh, was another glimmering sphere woven into the fabric of her memory. Not only had they beaded regalia together, but it was the most beautiful regalia she'd ever seen—beautiful like the original shimmering jingle dress dancing its way into the dreams of her Ancestors. Now it was slipping away.

"Waawaate is my best friend," Bugz said. "Maybe my only friend." She wiped tears from her eyes.

"I'm your friend." Stormy looped a hair tie around the end of the braid she'd finished.

"Really?"

"No, I'm just using you to get to Waawaate." They both burst out laughing and Stormy set to work braiding the rest of Bugz's hair.

CHAPTER 50

In the Floraverse, the rain fell sideways, forcing Mishipizhiw to squint. Bugz rode, blinded, on his back. A few times already, they'd narrowly avoided another encounter with Clan:LESS. Still, a final showdown with their mortal foes seemed inevitable.

Worse yet, Bugz feared she wouldn't see the attack coming.

Bugz planned to rebuild her defenses. She envisioned creating an army of buffalo to storm across the prairies and join with a rebuilt fleet of Thunderbirds and an armada of sturgeon. But she didn't have access to the nest at the bottom of Lake of the Torches to bring these visions to life. Without that, she needed time. And time was yet another thing she didn't have.

Bugz had been on the run ever since Feng led Clan:LESS to her, with never more than a few hours' rest before she had to move again . . . barely enough time to turn on her bot and sleep, never mind rebuild a supernatural army. Exhaustion settled in. *This is what my Ancestors must've felt like,* Bugz thought to herself. She chuckled and shook her head as she realized she'd compared her pursuit through the Floraverse with the real-life genocide of the Americas. At least she could still laugh. *Better than crying.*

The rain came down in sheets as Mishi-pizhiw approached a peninsula beyond which lay Castle Rock, a natural stone formation that rose several hundred feet into the sky. It looked almost like a proto-skyscraper shaped from massive columns of rock. Time for one last push forward. They passed the final corner, trees and rocks flying by on the shore.

A massive flotilla of Clan:LESS warships, helicopters, and submarines waited for them in the bay. Scores of mega–Gatling guns lined the decks of aircraft carriers. All the way up Castle Rock stood countless tanks and turrets with guns trained on the water. Ever more helicopters continued to descend on the bay. Whatever firepower Clan:LESS had wielded at the last battle had increased a hundredfold. They'd armed themselves to the teeth.

Mishi-pizhiw roared, partially to warn Bugz of the danger ahead and partially from pure exasperation. *How did I miss this?* Bugz wondered. *The balance really has shifted.* Bugz felt a tingling sensation orbit her spine, her paranoia manifest. She turned to look back over her shoulder. Dozens of choppers descended from the sky, boxing Bugz and Mishi-pizhiw in.

"It's going to take one helluva miracle for us to get out of here alive!" Bugz yelled to Mishi-pizhiw. He grunted in response. "Well, let's not make it easy on them." She gripped his head tightly and the giant horned serpent dove beneath the surface of the water. The submarines descended and fired torpedoes in Bugz's direction.

The battle began.

CHAPTER 51

Bugz steered Mishi-pizhiw away from the submarines and the barrage hit his long torso, inflicting little damage. He dove even deeper, a leviathan lurking beneath the submarine fleet, and began to pick up speed. With a quick turn, he rose and rammed the first sub into the second, into the third, and so on—until he had shattered them all like a tae kwon do master breaking planks of wood. He shook off the effects of the impact and swam toward the surface with Bugz still clinging to his back.

On the waves above, aircraft carriers circled the area around which Mishi-pizhiw prepared to emerge. The helicopter gunners trained their weapons on the same spot. Alpha descended from one of the turrets on Castle Rock to watch the carnage up close. A hush fell over the Clan:LESS warriors. The calm before the storm. Even the rain stopped, and the sky began to clear.

Mishi-pizhiw shot straight up from the water and climbed a hundred feet in the air. At this height, he paused, appeared to defy gravity for a moment, and turned sideways before starting his descent. He planned to crash-land onto the ships beneath. The mega–Gatling guns fired, as did the helicopter gunships. Instantly, Bugz could see something was wrong. The guns were doing serious damage to Mishi-pizhiw's diamond plating. Clan:LESS had upgraded their weapons in a major way.

Mishi-pizhiw writhed in pain. He landed heavily, destroying one of the aircraft carriers and a few smaller boats in the process, but he appeared badly hurt. As the craft sunk, Mishi-pizhiw slithered toward land. Bugz turned on his back and fired both of her guns at the wreckage behind her. A few moments later, hundreds of gamertags rose from the sunken vessels.

"Mishi-pizhiw, you're going to make it through this." Bugz's voice cracked. In desperation, and remembering the teachings of the Sweat Lodge, Bugz beseeched the stones that littered the shore: "Grandmother, Grandfather." The rocks began to shake. They rose as Bugz conducted them into a swirling symphony above her head. With a gesture of her hands, she lobbed them toward the helicopters. They flew slowly and bounced off harmlessly as energy cannons fired back at her. "The rock thing is going to take me some time to master," she said to her few remaining viewers as she and Mishi-pizhiw reached the shore.

Bugz jumped down from Mishi-pizhiw and the pair tore off along the beach beneath Castle Rock. Helicopters flew over the treetops and fired on them. Bugz picked off the pilots one by one, but the gunners worked too fast. They pelted Mishi-pizhiw mercilessly. He shook furiously, transforming into his land form, and ran back along the beach and up the side of the mountain. He pounced on tanks along the way, throwing the wreckage down to the lake.

Bugz froze for a second as she watched the beast's awesome beauty. The sight of Alpha slowly training his energy cannon on Mishi-pizhiw snapped her out of it.

"No!" She fired off several shots that knocked Alpha back. As Mishi-pizhiw turned to see what the commotion was about, helicopter gunfire crashed near Bugz and knocked her down.

Mishi-pizhiw bounded down Castle Rock, taking fire and damage the whole way. Still, he snatched Bugz from the ground with his jaws and flung her onto his back. He ran through the shallows and leapt to the nearest aircraft carrier. He landed claws-first and tore up huge chunks of the tarmac. Then he leapt to the next carrier, leaving a similar trail of destruction before diving off into deeper waters.

Mishi-pizhiw transformed into his water form and spirited Bugz away. Under the cover of a massive forest of seaweed, he swam her to the far side of the bay. There, amid the roots of the lily pads and bulrushes, Mishi-pizhiw locked eyes with Bugz. His giant catlike pupils pierced the center of her soul.

Bugz thought of her mother. "I love you," she whispered. The tears welled in Bugz's eyes and dissolved in the virtual water of the lake. The giant beast motioned with his head for Bugz to stay.

"I'm coming with you," she protested. He simply shook his head no.

Bugz and Mishi-pizhiw nuzzled their noses together as they breathed deeply and exhaled, sending bubbles upward. Bugz shuddered to the core of her being. The beast smiled a final time, turned, and sped toward the battle.

From beneath the shallow waves, breathing through a water lily stalk so as not to send any more telltale bubbles to the surface, Bugz watched as Mishi-pizhiw launched a valiant assault on the Clan:LESS horde. The energy fire crashed into him as he roared to the heavens. He snatched a helicopter into his mouth and threw the chopper at another gunship, sending them both spiraling from the sky. He looped his serpentine body through the air over and over again, smashing dozens of boats and an aircraft carrier in the process. Through it all, his body was illuminated with gunfire and lasers. He coiled himself around his targets and dragged half a dozen tanks into the water with him. He surfaced and spun several times, taking more Clan:LESS machines with him as he corkscrewed through the air.

From Bugz's vantage point, the battle was all chaos: Mishi-pizhiw in motion, hundreds of gamertags flying to the sky, and the energy cannons raining fire down on her last remaining companion.

Under a massive barrage of fire, and with a dramatic roar that shook the earth, the greatest beast the Floraverse had ever known fell to the beach with a thunderous blow, finally spent. Mishi-pizhiw's eyes remained open, but they stared past Bugz as the energy cannons rained fire down on him for five minutes straight, interrupted only by the occasional rocket or torpedo. When the gunfire ended, Mishi-pizhiw's dark form lay motionless, half ashore and half in the water, still smoldering. Tears flowed from Bugz's eyes, turning the shallows in which she lay to salt water.

Bugz remained submerged, breathing through the stalk as members of Clan:LESS took selfies with the body. She watched as the flotilla broke up and searched for her. She stayed hidden as they loaded the turrets, helicopters, and submarines onto the aircraft carriers and sailed away. She watched the sun set. She saw the moon rise. Finally, after what felt like an eternity underwater, she swam across the bay.

In the pale moonlight, Bugz walked slowly out of the water. The waves lapped gently against her legs as she approached her fallen friend. The reflection of the light above danced on the surf. She fell to her knees beside Mishi-pizhiw. She felt a sadness as old as life itself. She looked to the moon and felt only loneliness. Bugz looked back to the face of her old friend—one she'd created, and one who'd helped her rule this world. She caressed him softly.

Bugz kissed Mishi-pizhiw goodbye.

CHAPTER 52

The young men of Clan:LESS marched through the forest near the Rez wearing their lumberjack shirts and ripped jeans. Though they were not in the 'Verse, most of them still wore Ø tattoos on their arms as a nod to their virtual identities. Their phones, completely illuminated, lit the night. They'd travelled from across the continent to cement their victory. Now they aimed to conquer the final half of the nexus.

They alternated between chants of "She can never win! We must always win!" and "Clan! LESS! Clan! LESS!" Occasionally they'd break into boisterous yelling and laughter. Three dozen of them marched together. Though they represented only a small fraction of Clan:LESS's rapidly growing membership, these were the highest-ranking officers of the clan that was not a clan.

Finally, they pushed through the edge of the trees and

came to the clearing the Behemoth had stumbled into only nights before. They roared in approval and hoisted their fists to the sky.

One man, identifying himself as Gym—though considerably skinnier than his 'Versona—spoke up. "We've come here tonight to do one thing . . . finish the job!"

The mob roared.

"That's right!" Gym jumped up onto the Thunderbird's Nest and continued his speech. "We've already unlocked the power of unlimited resources in the 'Verse. And we've built up our skills. No one will ever catch up to us now." He examined his troops and nodded his head. "So let's destroy this monument to savagery! Let's destroy it before it falls into the wrong hands. Let's make our victory last forever!" He beat his chest.

This bravado seemed to mask the real reason they wanted to destroy the Thunderbird's Nest. The leaders of Clan:LESS had probably calculated they could not defend the real-world nest since it was so close to the Rez. They'd probably also figured any sort of sustained occupation would invite attention from the authorities, which they always wanted to avoid. So rather than contend with those problems, or allow anyone else to access the power of this sacred site, they'd decided to destroy it. "Let's go!"

The horde yelled their approval and began demolishing the Thunderbird's Nest. They produced crowbars and worked in large teams to flip the biggest rocks and roll them away. The remaining soldiers grabbed smaller stones and threw them into the forest. They screamed and yelled. It was exhausting work, even for such a large group. One stone, boulder, and rock at a time, they destroyed the monument built by the Anishinaabe Ancestors thousands of years before.

Bugz, surprised to see anyone in her place of solace, ran into the clearing. In the moonlight, she saw the desecration up close. She froze with rage.

Before she could speak, Gym put his arm around Bugz's shoulder and faked a smile. He called to the crowd, "Well, well, well, look who we have here! You'll never guess who's come to protect their secret hideout." He played up the theatrics for the crowd. "What an honor!"

"It's Bugz!" an unseen clan member yelled from the darkness.

"What do you say we get some payback on our little Bugz here, shall we?" With his arm still around Bugz, he walked her to a large nearby rock. With dozens of Clan:LESS members surrounding her, Bugz trembled. She didn't know what to do other than go along with her tormentors. Gym sat down with her on a stone as wide across as a park bench. "What do you think, boys? She doesn't look so scary in real life, does she?"

"No, she doesn't!" a voice yelled.

"She's chubby," said another.

"Classic catfish."

Bugz held her breath as she struggled against Gym's grip. Looking around, she couldn't see a path to escape. The horde was circling her now. She shook her shoulders free from his arm.

"Whoa! We've got a live one!" Gym yelled. As Bugz stood to run away, three other members of Clan:LESS stepped forward to box her in along with Gym. As they inched closer and closer, Bugz unleashed a primal yell. She trembled, terrified the goons would hurt her. More Clan:LESS soldiers stepped forward to tighten the trap. She screamed again until her body shook.

"You're done," said a disembodied voice. The man scolding her stepped through the crowd. Two Clan:LESS soldiers parted to make way for him. "You're done." He repeated the phrase over and over until she stopped yelling. Her voice felt hoarse. Bugz feared for her life. The man brought his bearded face to within inches of her own. They locked eyes. *One green, one brown,* Bugz thought. She ran through her memories of the Floraverse. *Alpha.*

"You're done," Alpha said again, nodding his head. "We've got it all. We've destroyed this side of the nexus. We control the other side. We've killed your creatures."

"Help!" Bugz yelled.

"No one can hear you," Alpha continued, his mouth just inches from her face.

The horde egged him on.

"Get away from me," Bugz fumed.

Alpha grabbed her phone from her hands. He thrust it in her face. The phone scanned her features and, recognizing Bugz, unlocked itself. Alpha pulled the phone back and, with a few taps, deleted her Floraverse account. Everything she'd accomplished was gone. She lunged forward, but he sidestepped her and swiped through her messages.

"There, that wasn't so difficult now, was it?" Alpha grinned. "I don't want to hear you complain about starting over. We've all had to do it. Fair is fair."

The mob snickered.

"Screw you!" Bugz cried.

"Keep yelling," Alpha responded. "I want to see if anyone comes." He turned to examine his supporters. "Fellas, what do you think? Is anyone coming for her?" With a self-satisfied expression, he scanned the crowd. "I don't know what's sadder—the way she looks now or the fact the traitor ain't coming to save her."

The members of Clan:LESS laughed and turned to leave, high-fiving each other. Alpha tossed her phone into the dirt. The horde picked up their tools and marched back into the forest.

Bugz dove forward to grab her phone and collapsed against the largest boulder remaining in the clearing. She could still hear the clan whooping and chanting her name as the voices and phone flashlights disappeared into the darkness. Through tears, she raised her phone. She already knew her 'Versona and everything it unlocked was erased, but she held out hope that some part of the nest's power remained. She set up a new account, launched AR mode, and examined the ruins that littered the clearing.

Her screen showed nothing. Not even a spark. The magic was gone.

CHAPTER 53

Feng stared at the basic 'Versona on the screen of his phone. No muscles, no guns, no Clan:LESS tattoo. This is what Bugz had reduced him to. He checked his messages and saw they were still full of hate mail. He sighed in frustration and tossed the phone on the couch beside him.

Liumei stood up from the table where she'd been reviewing digital medical forms. "Everything alright?"

"It's fine." Feng leaned back with a scowl.

"Teenage heartbreak got you down?" Liumei said with a smile. She sat down on the far end of the couch.

"I don't love her. Not after what she did to me."

"Bugz has a lot going on, Feng. Her brother is sick."

"So you're taking her side?"

"No, I'm not taking sides, Feng. I'm just pointing it out." Liumei shifted to face Feng more fully. "So what happened?"

"She killed me." Feng paused to make sure Liumei understood he meant in the 'Verse. "It's messed up. It's the second time she's eliminated me. And like I told you before, it takes forever to get back to the Spirit World once you respawn. I'm basically a noob."

"Why'd she 'kill' you?" Liumei asked using air quotes.

"Clan:LESS destroyed everything she created online, and she claims I led them to her. But I didn't know they put a tracking device on me. She cut my head off!" Feng felt Liumei studying him. Self-consciously, he tried to relax his face to appear less angry.

Liumei spoke. "I don't know what most of that means, but I do know how much Bugz's creations meant to her." She brushed a few stray hairs from her eyes. "That must've really hurt her."

Feng sat silently.

"I just got a text. I've got to run to the hospital." Liumei stood and gathered her bag. Halfway out the door, she stopped and turned back to Feng. "Feng, I don't think she should've cut your head off. God, that sounds weird to say. But if you really care about her, you've got to work this out, together."

Feng huffed. With this, Liumei granted his wish and left him alone. He stewed in his thoughts a moment before reaching for his phone. Examining his pathetic 'Versona, he hatched a plan to accelerate his return to the Spirit World.

CHAPTER 54

Waawaate inhaled slowly, his body working hard to expand and contract his lungs. His brow furrowed above closed eyes. His chest paused at the height of his aspiration as though he strained to hear a message, some secret communication that might make his path easier. His body relaxed and slowly his torso sank back toward the hospital bed. A short pause and the cycle started again. He shifted in place and grunted with the effort.

A nurse pressed buttons and checked the readings on the various machines that pumped, whizzed, and whirred around Waawaate's body. She quickly scanned a chart and continued with her work.

"What happened?" Bugz asked, seated on the bed beside her brother's feet.

"It's one of the chemo drugs they gave him." Bugz's mom spoke up, appearing not to see anything except for the patch of hospital blanket immediately in front of her. "A really bad side effect. They switched the drug, but who knows at this point." She teared up and inhaled deeply. "Sing, Bugz. Sing that healing song you know."

Bugz looked to her feet and searched her memory. After a breath, her sharp, melodic voice cut through the stale, tense air in the hospital room. "Eniwek igo kiga'onji-pimaadiz ndiwe'igan . . . ," she began. *Through my drum you will live just that much more.* Bugz belted out the prayer song, absolutely shredding the air with a voice as clear and beautiful as it was pristine in its intention to make her brother well again. "Hey ya wey, ya eh, ya ho, we yo ho wey . . ." She punctuated each vocable with a burning desperation. Perhaps if she nailed this song, the Creator would have mercy on her brother. She sang the song four times through, more loudly and soulfully with each repetition.

When Bugz finished, the song's melody seemed to reverberate in the air for a second. Soon enough, though, it dissipated, leaving those assembled, including Waawaate, in silence. He did not move. His EKG pulsed. Finally, he stirred and woke slowly. Tears flowed to the brim of Bugz's eyes but did not fall down her cheek. Her eyes reddened. *Through my drum, you will live just a little bit longer.*

Bugz's father smiled. "Waawaate, you're a heck of a warrior, my boy."

"I could hear Bugz singing." Waawaate stretched with some effort. "Off-key." He laughed, and everyone else smiled.

"I'd tell you to shut up if you weren't so weak," Bugz replied, a genuine look of happiness spreading across her face.

"Still strong enough to take you out, even in the 'Verse." Suddenly, Waawaate grimaced.

"What's the matter, son?" Bugz's mother asked.

"Nothing, I just have no energy. Just talking and moving around, I feel totally—" He started to wheeze, and lost himself to a fit of dry coughs.

The nurse rubbed his back. "I'm going to see if we can give you something else to help with the pain." Waawaate nodded with his eyes closed as she exited the room, leaving the Holiday clan in silence.

Bugz's dad finally spoke. "You gotta watch that stuff. It can take you out. Too many painkillers."

"I tell you what, I never thought I'd say this, but that doesn't sound so bad right now," Waawaate responded. The smile disappeared from Bugz's face.

Her mother sighed and brushed the hair from Waawaate's forehead. "Don't talk like that, baby. You're fighting this and we're going to help you. But you've got to have hope."

"I do have hope, but it's tough. The medicine they gave me only made me sicker. The Anishinaabe medicine didn't help either. I don't want to give up, but I don't want to just fade away into nothing either."

Bugz's tears now found their way down her cheeks. One crept into her mouth. She registered the salty taste. It was easier to process that sensation than what her brother spoke of. Waawaate'd always been her hero, her protector, her source of laughs during a tough time. *And now here he is about to . . .* she refused to complete the thought.

"It's okay to feel like that, son," Bugz's dad said. "Back in the day, they actually had a traditional medicine for what you're talking about. The old ones would allow it in cert—"

"What?!" Bugz stood, fresh tears tracing a path on her cheeks. "How can you talk like that?"

"Relax, Buggy, I'm just trying to reassure him. You and your mom are always telling me to validate people's feelings first . . ."

Bugz turned and stormed out of the room.

"Of course I'm gonna tell him not to do it. He has to fight . . ." Frank's words trailed off as Bugz rounded the corner into the hospital hallway. She pulled out her phone. It reflected the neon lights overhead as she launched a messaging app.

"Can you meet me at the hospital?" Bugz texted Stormy.

"Yeah what's up?"

"I'll tell you when you get here ☹"

"Aww ☹"

CHAPTER 55

Feng walked into the clearing, stunned by what he saw. The Thunderbird's Nest was no more. One large rock lay near a tree, another at the edge of the woods. Smaller stones were strewn everywhere. He wondered for a moment whether he was lost, but he pulled out his phone and confirmed this was where the nest should've been. He couldn't believe it.

Feng scanned the entirety of the clearing through his phone to confirm the damage. Where once this place had pulsed with ribbons of energy so intense they lit up his phone's entire screen, now he could see nothing. The respawn point was no more. Feng realized, with some disappointment, he'd have to find another way to accelerate his 'Versona's return to the Spirit World.

As he lowered his phone, another thought entered his head. He pictured himself working tirelessly for the rest of the day to reassemble the stone circle.

Quickly, and with seemingly divine inspiration, Feng jogged to the large stone near the tree and tried to lift it. Nothing. He crouched beside it and tried to push it. His feet slid away from the stone and he nearly fell forward. He chastised himself for lacking Herculean strength. He found a large stick nearby and tried to use it as a lever to roll the rock over. He grunted. Just as he felt he might move the stone, the stick snapped and nearly impaled him. Hopping to the side of the splintering wood, Feng sighed at the truth. He would not assemble the Thunderbird's Nest on this day. He gained a new respect for Bugz's Ancestors.

Feng wiped his brow and looked to the sky. A cloud cast a long shadow over him. Suddenly, the rays of the sun burst through the cloud and shone brilliantly. For a fraction of a second, he could not see. But when his vision returned, he was moved.

A feeling formed in the pit of Feng's stomach as he examined the cloud ensnaring the sun. In its center, as though pierced, was a hole through which the light shone. A moment later, the wind carried the cloud forward. It obscured the sun and covered the land in shadow again. Nonetheless, Feng knew what it meant.

A hole in the day.

As the wind picked up, Feng decided to make things right with Bugz. He turned and ran back toward the Rez.

CHAPTER 56

As Bugz approached the hospital exit, she pictured Waawaate smiling. She pictured them dancing at a pow-wow together. She pictured beadwork. She pictured flames consuming her happy memories, leaving only ash and pain behind. The doors slid apart and the cool damp air wrapped itself around her. Stormy arrived a short time later.

"How's it going?" she asked.

Bugz shook her head in response. The corners of her mouth became too heavy to lift. She didn't want to speak. She just kept shaking her head.

"Aww, you poor thing." Stormy pulled her in for a hug. Tears welled in Stormy's eyes too. As they walked across the street to the picnic table, Stormy reached for Bugz's hand. Bugz felt the warmth of her touch and thought of Feng. She shook her head as Stormy led her to the table and sat down.

They reminisced about Waawaate. They repeated the cheap joke Chalice had made at the pow-wow about whistling at the northern lights. They laughed at Stormy's genuine fear of someone calling the aurora down to earth.

"'Member? You were so scared," Bugz said through smiling eyes.

"Don't even start!"

Their laughter trailed off. Bugz felt a looming dread creeping up behind her.

"It's so messed up that he wants to leave us . . . ," Bugz observed herself saying. "I mean, of anyone on the Rez, Waawaate is the one out of all of us who is *actually* living. He should live forever."

"You're right about that," Stormy murmured. She sighed.

"What?" Bugz noticed something in the other girl's demeanor.

"Nothing."

"No, you look like you're thinking of something."

Stormy paused for too long to be able to dismiss the idea. The dread crept closer.

"What is it?" Bugz asked.

"Do you believe what the old people say about onjine? About patai'itiwin?"

"What do you mean?"

"Like onjine means karma, right? And patai'itiwin is karma too, except what goes around comes back around to your kid instead of you?"

"What are you getting at, Stormy?"

"Just . . . I heard my grandma and some others talking about Waawaate being sick. They were saying it's because your dad used to be pretty bad when he was younger. Fights and stuff. Drinking. Do you ever wonder if . . ." Stormy slowed as a scowl settled on Bugz's face. "Never mind. Forget I said anything."

Bugz thought for a moment. "That's messed up, Stormy. My dad would never do anything to hurt Waawaate." In spite of the defense she mounted, a seed of doubt had been planted in Bugz's mind. "I'm gonna go for a walk. Sorry to waste your time."

"No, I'm sorry. I shouldn't have said anything." Stormy scanned Bugz's expression. "I'll wait here for a bit in case you want to talk some more."

Bugz walked across a gravel parking lot opposite the picnic table. She noticed her father's empty truck parked with the windows rolled down. Her memory of how he'd counseled her brother about making his final journey played on the raw wound Stormy had just inflicted.

"Hey, Buggy," her father's voice called out behind her. She turned to face Frank.

"Don't call me that. You know I hate it." She glared at her father, wishing her eyes were capable of shooting lasers.

"I'm sorry."

"Everything was bad and you made it worse." Bugz seethed. The look of bewilderment on Frank's face only made her angrier. "And instead of helping, you're talking to Waawaate about dying?"

"I . . . I didn't say that."

"Why did you say anything?" Bugz turned and stomped off. She heard Frank's footsteps behind her. "Stay the hell away from me."

"I know you're mad, but can we just talk?"

"Talking ain't going to help the way I'm feeling right now!"

Bugz bolted for the tree line at the edge of the parking lot. But her father chased after her and, when he caught up, wrapped her in a bear hug. She thought of the Clan:LESS horde that had cornered her in the forest. She struggled against him furiously and broke free.

"Get off, get off, get off!" she shouted. Her father glanced nervously at Stormy, who was watching from a distance. "Get away from me!" Bugz shouted again. "I hate you!"

Bugz hated how he'd grabbed her; she hated everything about how she felt right now. Her father stepped forward.

"Stop!" Bugz yelled. Frank ignored her. "If you come any closer, I swear . . ." She pulled her knife out and held it to her forearm. She thought of her cousin Ally. Frank stopped in his place. Bugz could see the tears forming in his eyes. He bit his lower lip.

Bugz studied her father. For a split second, she felt sorry for him. But her pain swallowed her again. Pain for her brother, pain for Feng, pain for losing the way things were just a short time ago.

She turned and ran into the dark forest.

CHAPTER 57

A resolute Bugz plunged her carving knife into the bark of a cedar tree. She peeled the outer bark and ran the knife along the trunk to tear off a long strip of inner bark that resembled a six-foot piece of string. She reached as high as she could and cut off another strip. As she peeled the long, thin stretches of bark from the tree, she exposed the wet, naked core beneath. Bugz set the ribbon of inner bark aside and peeled off another, then another, and another still. She had to work deliberately because the bark peeled much slower now than it would've in the spring. This gave her time to listen to the thoughts swirling in her head.

After Bugz had collected a score of these bark streamers, she carried them into the clearing where the Thunderbird's Nest had once stood. It was now just a small field pockmarked with seemingly random rocks and stones. She sat on top of a large gray fragment of a boulder. She carefully selected three strips of cedar and tossed the rest into a pile within arm's reach in the tall grass beside her. She lined up the tops and began to braid.

As Bugz's fingers navigated between the strips of bark—pushing, pulling, and weaving on autopilot—she let herself relax. The repetitive task set her mind free. She wondered whether her dad really meant to counsel Waawaate to take a shortcut to the Spirit World. She wondered why Feng had lashed out at her. She wondered what her brother could do to heal himself.

If each bead laid into a piece of beadwork was a prayer, Bugz decided that each twist of the braids she tied could represent one of her memories. She remembered all of the beautiful moments she and her brother had shared. She picked up more strips of bark and wove them into the pattern of the braid, both lengthening it and ensuring its strength. She thought of her family and her parents, and worried they'd never be the same if her brother didn't recover. She completed weaving a strand of braided bark more than twenty feet long and placed it next to her on the rock. She drew three more strips of bark from the pile, lined up the tops, and began braiding those as well. She tried to picture a future without Waawaate, but she couldn't see anything. The thick fibers calloused her hands.

Bugz thought of Feng. She felt a pang of hurt wrestling her from her zen state. *Why did he betray me?* She grimaced.

Why did he pile on like everyone else? Bugz noticed she'd tensed up. She took a deep breath, exhaled, and returned to braiding. She shook her head at the ideas she'd held of Feng. Simple ideas of him being a man she could trust. One to live up to the example set by her father and her brother, or at least the examples she'd believed in earlier. The infallible father. The invincible older brother. Even those notions now disappeared from her mind like sand eroded from the earth. She added more strips to the braid. She happily remembered the beautiful ride she and Feng had taken through the Floraverse, all laughs, flower power, and fun. She finished braiding this chain and placed it next to the first. An image of this rope hanging from a tree flashed in her mind. She studied the cords she'd already completed.

Bugz thought of the Floraverse. She withdrew three more strips of bark, lined up their tops, and started braiding again. She thought back to the first time she'd realized she could respawn at will, in this very spot. It felt so long ago, though only a couple of years had passed since then. She'd come here to get some quiet after someone at school said something racist to her. She hadn't felt like telling her parents because they would've turned it into some big thing. Meetings, phone calls, standing up for yourself. Bugz didn't want to be a hero that day; she just wanted to get away from the hurt. Instead, she found her destiny: a source of nearly unlimited power. She wove more strips of bark into the braid. Within a few weeks of her discovery, she'd figured out how to bend the Floraverse to her will. And a few weeks after that, she'd built many of her creatures. Soon, the views on her streams took off, and the money and fame followed. *It's all gone now.* She laid down her newest braid.

Bugz collected the three braids and examined them from top to bottom, pulling on them length-wise to test their strength. She lined up their tops and tied the bundle together with a shorter piece of bark. She weaved the three braids together, working slowly, diligently, and with great focus.

Bugz's thoughts traveled to the Floraverse. She flew over Lake of the Torches again. She saw flames burning contentedly along the shores. Everywhere she looked, her creatures lived again in her mind's eye. Sturgeon swam leisurely amidst the black waves. Thunderbirds swooped back and forth in the sky. Scores of animals frolicked along the beach. In the center of it all was Mishi-pizhiw, corkscrewing his serpentine body over and over again in a never-ending loop of pure joy. She'd raised Mishi-pizhiw as her first creation and had invested every new insight and technique she learned from the Floraverse into his development. He was the pinnacle of her prowess and the greatest recipient of her affection. "My baby," she caught herself whispering. She finished braiding the strands together and examined her creation.

Bugz held the thick cedar rope in her hand. It looked like sisal, cowboy rope, right down to the frayed edges.

She ran her hand over its rough contours and pulled on it hard. It had very little give. Bugz sighed. She felt an unrelenting ache at the center of her soul. She wanted it to end.

Bugz thought again of her cousin Ally. She took her curved knife and sliced into the skin above her bicep. She gasped, grimaced, and shut her eyes tight as she pulled the blade forward. She stopped and dropped the knife. She couldn't continue. Bugz exhaled slowly through clenched teeth as the searing hurt coursed through her body. She felt tears run down her face. She hated herself so much for doing this. It felt wrong. With blood trickling down her arm, Bugz looked to the sky and shuddered as she exhaled a long, soft cry.

CHAPTER 58

Feng walked up the gravel driveway to Frank and Summer's house, rubbing his hands nervously. He could feel his stomach somersaulting through his T-shirt. He made his way up the steps, steadying himself against the guardrail. He replayed the speech inside his head again for the millionth time. *Just say sorry. No matter what she says, just keep saying sorry.* He took a deep breath and reached out to knock. *No. Tell her you love her. Like family. You've never felt this before and . . . like family? That's terrible. Just tell her you love her and that's it. No, just tell her you're sorry.*

"Feng?" Frank opened the door, looking worried. "What are you doing here? Bugz said we wouldn't see you too much anymore."

"That's why I'm here." Feng's voice trembled. "I want to make it right."

"Listen, I'm sure you can work it out, but right now I need your help. Bugz took off and . . . it was bad," Frank said. "I've been driving around for hours. I have no idea where she is. I talked to everyone on the Rez. Stormy. Her mom. Nobody's seen her." Frank sighed. "Waawaate's getting worse. I'm really worried."

"Why?"

Frank's mouth appeared to sour.

"What did she say?"

"I don't know," Frank said. Feng could tell he was trying to stifle tears. "I'm just worried . . . I don't want her to be alone."

"Like self-harm?"

Frank refused to answer.

"I think I know where she is," Feng said. "I was just there."

"Okay, let me grab my keys."

As Frank disappeared inside the doorway, Feng turned and ran. He was at the end of the driveway before Frank could yell after him.

"Wait!"

It was too late. Feng ran straight into the forest behind the houses on the far side of the road. Feng could hear Frank's tires spinning in the gravel in the distance, but he knew he'd put too much distance between the two of them. Feng felt like it was all up to him now.

The sun set.

CHAPTER 59

With her cut arm stinging, Bugz stood and walked to the tallest cottonwood tree at the edge of the clearing. She looked up to the branches. She'd expected cutting to make her feel so much better. That's what her cousin told her—that it felt good to feel something—but all Bugz felt now was guilt and sorrow. It didn't make anything better. This felt nothing like the sacrifice she'd seen her father and others make at the Sundance. When they were cut, the whole community watched. It became holy, a selfless act. What she'd done here alone felt only selfish. Bugz's world continued to spin out of control around her.

Bugz took the rope she'd made and tied it in a loop. She suddenly recognized what she'd created—she'd braided a noose. The realization scared her.

As though on autopilot, Bugz walked to the tree, wrapped the free end of the cord around the tree trunk, and threw the noose over a thick branch. She stared at the rope dangling from the monstrous cottonwood. It looked so ominous. She trembled. *This isn't who I am.*

In the ocean of her heart and in the land of her spirit, a deep rumbling began, and it drove Bugz forward. Her brother. Her father. Feng. Stormy. Mishi-pizhiw. The nest. Clan:LESS. All of her feelings cascaded and roiled with an unstoppable momentum. In her head, she knew she didn't want to harm herself any more than she already had. But the force of this moment in her life propelled Bugz on. She held the noose in her hands as she walked backward, away from the tree, like a child playing tug-of-war.

Bugz looked up at the branch and took a deep breath. She closed her eyes and tried to picture the end result of the course she was on. She could not. Teardrops raced down her cheeks. She wondered whether anyone was looking for her and whether they would find her in time. *Who will it be?*

Bugz said a prayer in Ojibwe. She mumbled the words as her breath shuddered under the weight of tears. *Ni-noonde-pimaadiz, I want to live.* She completed her prayer and spoke to Waawaate.

"I want to see you again."

Bugz stood motionless. The evening summer breeze picked up and rustled through the tall grasses on the edge of the clearing.

"Brother," Bugz said.

CHAPTER 60

Sister, Waawaate replied in his mind, miles away. They'd sedated him and moved him into an intensive care unit. To the nurse caring for him, he appeared as though in a fever dream. Though intubated, he tossed and turned in the hospital bed. The nurse checked his vital signs. He grimaced.

In his mind's eye, Waawaate stood surrounded by cottonwood leaves in a cold and gray Sundance arbor. He looked to the tree and saw its dry, dead branches clawing the sky. He turned. Bugz stood in front of him. Her arms were marked for the piercing ceremony. He found himself trapped in the mirror image of Bugz's Sundance dream.

Waawaate looked to his hand and saw he was holding a scalpel. He walked to Bugz. He knew she expected him to cut her, but he didn't want to. Waawaate reached out and pinched the side of Bugz's shoulder, gathering skin and fat between his thumb and index finger. Her flesh felt elastic.

It would be hard for her skin to break. She would suffer. Waawaate looked back to Bugz's face. They made eye contact and held each other's gaze for what felt like a long time. She stared straight ahead at the craggy tree in the center of the darkened Sundance circle. A tear flowed from her eye and traced its way slowly down her cheek.

Waawaate raised the sisal rope that would tie her to the tree. It ended in a noose. He panicked. This wasn't right. She needed a forked rope. A noose was a bad sign. He had to cut the loop in half.

Waawaate took the scalpel and tried to cut the rope, but he couldn't. He struggled and struggled but couldn't find the strength to sever the braided cord. He felt weak and powerless. He couldn't escape this nightmare.

As Waawaate struggled to cut the noose, his hair fell forward. Still focused on moving the blade through the sisal, he blew the hair from his face. He stopped for a second and looked to the darkened sky above. He blew through his lips again and whistled a traditional melody, watching the sky spring to life.

In his hospital room, the nurse watched with concern as Waawaate struggled against the ventilator tube in his mouth. He puckered his lips and blew and blew, appearing to try to blow the tube out of his body.

CHAPTER 61

At the Thunderbird's Nest, Bugz closed her eyes and saw her brother miles away. It devastated her to see him like this, a shell of his former self, with a tube running down his throat.

"Help me," she asked of the image in her mind.

Waawaate leaned forward slightly and attempted to blow the tube from his mouth. It was so sad.

"I'm praying for you, brother. Pray for me too. I need your help."

He puckered his lips again and blew harder.

Bugz shook her head. "I'm selfish to ask you for help. You're suffering so much."

He made the blowing gesture a third time. Bugz furrowed her brow, eyes still closed. In her mind, Waawaate's breath caught the edge of the ventilator tube and made a faint noise. She realized he wasn't trying to blow. He was trying to whistle. He just couldn't find the tone with his mouth and airway blocked.

The tears returned and pulled the sides of Bugz's mouth toward the ground. It made it harder for her to form her lips into the proper shape. Bugz struggled to move her jaw to the right position. Somehow, she smiled. Her brother had come through for her again, just like he always had.

Still standing alone in the clearing with her eyes squeezed shut, Bugz finally pursed her lips and let out a very soft whistle. She blew harder and harder until the sound of the whistle pierced the stillness of the forest. She blew through the whistle until all of the air escaped her lungs. She closed her eyes.

She heard someone whistling back.

CHAPTER 62

Feng sprinted through the forest toward the clearing. Through the distant cedars and cottonwoods, he saw Bugz. She stood holding a rope in her hands. But in his panic and from this distance, his mind couldn't make sense of the scene. He imagined he saw Bugz hanging. Tears flooded his eyes. *I'm not going to make it,* he told himself. *I won't be able to save her.* He sprinted harder. His lungs burned, but he pushed through it. He heard her make a very gentle sound in the distance, a soft whistle. He shuddered as the whistle grew louder and louder. He picked up the pace once more as he realized the meaning behind the sound.

Bugz was calling for help.

As Feng ran at full sprint, he ripped the eagle whistle from under his shirt and blew it as hard as he could. He took a deep breath, still running, and blew on the whistle again and again. The shrill noise pierced the night sky, peaking high above the clouds. As he blew on it harder, the pitch rose and flew even higher into the heavens.

High above the clearing, the northern lights roared to life. The clouds parted and the aurora borealis stretched its arms across the sky. Iridescent storm clouds rolled in from another dimension and enveloped the forest. Their green glow cast everything in an eerie, shimmering light. As the northern lights grew, they lowered themselves to the earth like a Day-Glo fog. As they descended from their heavenly perch, they transformed from green to pink. The spots that appeared to burn brightest turned white and smoldered with pink and purple. The Ancestors danced.

Feng kept blowing the whistle as he ran closer to the clearing. Suddenly, the electric storm illuminated his face with a flash of light and blinded him. When his sight returned, he could see figures. The Ancestors. Feng wasn't running anymore. Nothing moved except the northern lights around him.

In the glowing clouds, Feng saw his parents. Their features took shape in the luminescent shroud: his mother's loving eyes, the very eyes he'd first stared into as a newborn; his father's rugged, smiling face. He remembered how the stubble tickled him when they used to hug so long ago. As the light cascaded around him, he drew closer to their embrace. He felt something release within himself.

"Mother," Feng said. "Father."

"Farouq." His mother said. Feng's chest expanded. The apparition of his mother had spoken his birth name. His heart beat faster at hearing it again. He'd been called Farouq until he'd been taken from his home. He could still remember the exact moment at the re-education center when they'd renamed him "Feng." He was overcome, but he managed to ask the question that had tormented him for years.

"Why did you let them take me away from you?" The lump in Feng's throat made it difficult for him to speak. "It was so hard without you."

"We had no choice, Farouq," his mother said.

"They took us to the prison camp, my boy," the vision of his father spoke. "The same day, the authorities came to our house and told the rest of the family we'd abandoned you. That's when they took you away."

Feng's mother cried now at the memory, her tears refracting the northern lights in an infinite number of directions. "We never stopped looking for you. We never stopped thinking of you. We never stopped praying for you. We never forgot about you, not even for one minute."

Finally, the tears fell down Feng's cheek.

"I know it was hard on you, my son. It was hard on us too. Our only child, taken from us. The two of us imprisoned, neither one of us able to protect you." Feng's father shook his head, dispersing some of the green and purple waves around him. He grimaced.

"But why didn't you just give up? Why didn't you just tell them what they wanted to hear? You could've just said you didn't believe in Allah. You could've just said you'd learn Mandarin. They would've let you go and I could've come home . . ." Feng was having more and more difficulty speaking.

"Baby, Farouq. Don't you think if it were that simple, we would've done it?" His mother's pleading face left Feng feeling anguished. "We would've said anything to see you again."

The northern lights tightened their embrace around Feng, drawing the images of his parents in closer and closer. He lowered his head and gave his heart over to their warmth.

"They tried to take everything away from us. They took our freedom. They took our home. They even took you from us, our only son," Feng's father said. "But there is one thing they could never take away from us . . ."

The aurora loosened its grip and slowly lowered Feng back to reality. His mother spoke.

"We still love you."

CHAPTER 63

Bugz opened her eyes. For a brief moment, she wondered where she was. She no longer heard whistling. She could only see light. Her heart still ached. Her mind still worried. *This can't be heaven.* She blinked hard, attempting to reset her vision. She could see the northern lights cascading around her.

The aurora hugged Bugz, wrapping her in its glowing arms.

"It feels so good to be held by you." Bugz felt warmth. She felt the grief, anxiety, and heartache leave her body. For a moment, she felt ready to give in. But just as quickly, something returned to her.

Bugz's mind cleared. She could see only the rope, the tree, and the northern lights dancing around her. Waawaate may have helped her, but she knew she had to go the rest of the way herself. She picked up her carving knife and tore through the looped end of the cedar rope, severing it. Bugz examined the now forked rope in her hand. In an instant, she'd transformed it from a noose to a Sundance rope, from a harbinger of death to a symbol of life.

Bugz held the rope in her hands. She breathed deeply and smelled the fresh, sharp scent of the bark in the air. *Bagonegiizhigok. Hole in the cedar.* Bugz closed her eyes and spoke to her brother again.

"Thank you, Waawaate."

CHAPTER 64

Feng broke free from his vision, ran into the clearing, and rushed toward Bugz. He remained so caught in the moment that he didn't realize Bugz was simply standing there holding one end of a Sundance rope. He thought she still needed his help, that she still needed to be saved.

Feng tripped during his final steps and stumbled toward her. As he reached for her legs, a surprised Bugz lost her balance and fell backward. Though Feng tried to play hero and catch her, they fell awkwardly together and landed in a heap on the ground.

CHAPTER 65

Bugz opened her eyes and saw Feng's staring back at her. She smiled at him and remained in his arms as she slowly regained her bearings. Her head ached from the fall. Feng's clumsy diving catch had caught her completely off guard. Yet apart from a few aches and pains, she was mostly okay. She sat up and asked, "What happened?"

"Um." Feng wiped the tears from his eyes and smiled back at her. "I saved you." He glanced away.

"It doesn't feel too good when you save me." Bugz smiled, rubbing her head. "Besides, I sort of remember saving myself. So what were you doing?" She laughed.

"Well, I tried to save you," Feng said sheepishly. "But I guess . . . I was late."

"Oh god, typical dude. Shows up late to claim the credit."

"No, no."

"Listen, bud." Bugz affected a slight know-it-all tone to tease Feng. "I'm the hero of my own story. I had my own journey, my own moment of self-actualization, fulfilment, whatever, and now I'm about to go kick butt on my own behalf to make my own epic ending. Got it?"

Feng nodded with a smirk. He rubbed his elbow.

Bugz noticed and dropped the sarcastic tone. "Are you okay? Did I hurt you?" She paused for a second to watch Feng try to play the tough guy and shake his head. "Oh god, I did hurt you." She almost asked if she was too fat for him to catch her, but as she opened her mouth to speak, Bugz stopped herself. She thought of her skin in the 'Verse. She thought of how different she looked right now. Chubby, crying, hair probably a mess. And yet the boy was still here, still trying to hold her.

Bugz wiped her eyes. "I feel completely exposed. I can't believe you saw all of this." Bugz looked at the cut she'd given herself. "You must think I'm crazy and messed up and weird." She felt a drop of blood trickle down her arm. She sniffed. "But you're still here."

Feng nodded.

"Why?" Bugz asked.

"Because I wanted to see you again," Feng said.

Bugz thought of what he'd said to her in the school hallway.

"I wanted to see the real you," Feng said, apparently recalling the same moment. "I'm sorry for what I said before. Really, really sorry. That's not how I feel. You're beautiful. Inside, and out." He looked away. "That sounds cheesy." Feng sighed.

Bugz looked him up and down. "It's like you said: talking to women has never been your strong suit." She laughed as she told him she was just kidding. "What about you? You look like you've been crying too."

"Nah, I'm good." Feng rubbed his eyes, self-conscious now. "I was just thinking about my parents. I don't even know if they're still alive or not."

Bugz took his hand.

"But now I feel like I've got them right here with me, no matter what." Feng tapped his chest.

"That's a good way to think about it." Bugz stared at the cottonwoods lining the far side of the clearing.

"I've never felt the way I do about you about anyone before," Feng said, studying Bugz.

"I hate what you did to me," Bugz said, inhaling sharply. "Bringing Clan:LESS to my doorstep." She exhaled hard, blowing the hair away from her eyes in the process. "What really, really bothers me though is that when I needed you, instead of trying to help . . . you tried your best to hurt my feelings." Bugz grew pensive. "You really did hurt me."

A bird sang.

"But I still care for you," Bugz said.

"I'm sorry."

"I know. I'm sorry too."

Feng studied his sneakers for a second. "For what?"

"I'm sorry for killing you." Bugz chuckled. Deliberately, she drew in a deep breath.

Bugz pulled her phone from her pocket and launched a window into the 'Verse. Her eyes widened and were lit up by her screen. "Whoa!" Bugz turned her screen toward Feng, revealing the completely illuminated display. According to the AR, the area coursed with energy in the Floraverse. Bugz smiled.

Feng opened his mouth in awe. "It's back!"

Bugz nodded, eyes wide. Feng reached for his phone. He confirmed the return of the energy, lowered his screen and returned his eyes to Bugz. "You think maybe it wasn't ever a glitch on the map? You think maybe it was just you all along?" he asked. She shook her head.

"It's Waawaate. I know it." Bugz moved her character through the nest and respawned into the Spirit World. "I don't know how he did it, but the nexus is back." Bugz beamed. She raised her eyebrows and looked to Feng. "Now I can 'eliminate' you again anytime I want, right?" Their laughter outmatched her cheap joke and echoed in the hollow spaces across the clearing. Their smiles faded slowly. They sat together in silence for a long time, examining the stones slowly settling into the yellow grass beneath them.

"So what should we do next?" Feng asked. "Should we ride into the Floraverse? Should we launch a crusade against Clan:LESS? Should we take back what's rightfully yours?" Bugz felt him studying her, the blood still wet on her arm. "Should we go to the hospital?" he asked.

"We could." Bugz snuggled closer to Feng. "Or we could just stay here . . ." She inspected the eagle whistle around his neck again. She could feel Feng's breath. She smelled Axe body spray. "With each other." Bugz looked at Feng's lips and slowly raised her eyes to meet his. She felt a supernova exploding in her chest. She leaned closer, their lips about to touch.

Bugz paused. Suddenly, she felt something deeper than desire. A hunger came charging up from the depths and broke its way through to the surface. It was a drive to make things right, to settle unfinished business, to answer the call of destiny. She looked at her phone.

"I can't turn back now," Bugz said, as much to herself as to Feng. She raised her phone to her eyes and snapped it into headset mode. She nodded for Feng to follow suit. He did, and together they dove into the Floraverse.

Immersed in the Spirit World again, Feng followed Bugz to a cliff's edge high atop Castle Rock. A beautiful sunset exploded across the sky behind her. Bugz turned to face Feng, her sleek 'Versona of old replaced now by a figure that looked exactly the way she did in real life— beauty, imperfections, and all. Bugz smiled at Feng. She made the shape of a heart with her two hands. Slowly, she raised her two thumbs to the center of the heart until her hands became an infinity loop.

"This is the real me." Bugz brushed the hair from her eyes. "And I finally feel good about that."

Bugz embraced Feng and pulled him in. They kissed. As Feng closed his eyes and lost himself in the moment, Bugz gripped him by the scruff of his neck and threw him over the edge of the cliff. Bugz jumped high into the air, arcing into a perfect swan dive. As she dove down toward the Clan:LESS army, Bugz pulled her guns out and rained fire down on the enemy horde. Feng regained his composure, drew his weapons, and fell in closely behind Bugz as she sped toward the enemies below. A torrent of vines and animals tore down the rock face as Bugz summoned the life forms of the Floraverse to fight at her side once again. Even the rocks shook themselves loose from the bluffs and came roaring down behind her in a symphony of organized chaos.

As she dodged enemy fire and plunged into battle, Bugz wasn't sure how things would turn out. She didn't know if she'd win or lose. She didn't know if she was good enough or not. She didn't know if she and Feng would last forever.

She didn't know anything beyond that moment.

Still, for the first time in a long while she felt peace.

I am who I am,

In every world I walk in.

ACKNOWLEDGMENTS

Gichi-miigwech, a big thank you, to my beautiful wife, Lisa, for always having my back. To our fun, smart, and good-natured kids, Dominik, Bezh, and Tobasonakwut—I wrote this book for readers the ages you are now and will soon be. I hope you enjoy it. Miigwech also to my sister Shawon, who provided insight into and inspiration for the character Bugz. My mom and late father are always in my heart and mind, as are my sisters Diane, Kiizh, and Pat, as well as all of our extended family.

Ginanaakomininim, many thanks to you folks, the readers who put up with various drafts of this novel and really helped to make it much better, namely Ayat Mneina, Lisa, David Robertson, Waubgeshig Rice, Xiran Jay Zhao, Nahanni Fontaine, Sylvia Davis, Emily Coutts, Mark Rosner, and Tasha Spillett.

Many thanks as well to Lynne Missen and Peter Phillips,

who offered so many great notes, thoughtful suggestions, and ideas in conversation as we edited this. Thank you Linda Pruessen as well for your careful eye and helpful suggestions in the copyedit, and to Sarah Howden for the proofread. My deepest gratitude to my great literary agent Jackie Kaiser for paving the way for me to publish this book, and to Michael Levine and everyone at Westwood Creative Artists for your assistance along the way. Thanks also to Jack Leslie for giving me the opportunity to straighten my thoughts out about the story and themes of this novel. Thanks to Jay Soule for the beautiful cover art.

Gichi-miigwech to the late Gregory Younging for writing *Elements of Indigenous Style*, whose principles we tried to observe in the crafting of this book. Miigwech to Niigaan Sinclair and again to Tasha Spillett for some of the follow-up discussions on those points. Mársi cho to T'áncháy Redvers for the amazing help in compiling the culturally safe resources for youth and for all you've done to lead in that space. And of course to Senator Murray Sinclair for everything you've done to show the way and for providing the wisdom quoted in the epigraph. I would also like to thank Mehmet Tohti for the important work you do with the Uyghur Rights Advocacy Project.

Many thanks also to all the great people I've worked with in the book world to date for helping bring this opportunity about, including Nicole Winstanley, Diane Turbide, Stephen Myers, Evan Munday, Patrick Crean, Tara Mora,

Erin Balser, Ann Jansen, Shelagh Rogers, and the Canada Reads panelists and authors, among many others.

To the students at Pelican Falls, as I wrote in the dedication, I first started thinking about this book when I met some of you a few years back and noticed many of you reading YA novels. The young women at Pelican seemed to be reading a lot in particular. I wanted to put something together that you could see yourselves in but also imagine yourselves as becoming more than, if that makes sense. The world is a wonderful place, your communities are powerful, and you can hold your head high with pride in any world you choose to walk in. I hope this book helps you on your journeys as you seek your dreams.

To everyone else—all of us who wonder, worry, or otherwise dream of how things might be if we were a little more perfect—I hope this book helps somehow. Life is awesome and I hope we all live it to the fullest.

On a personal level I am very grateful to have the opportunity to publish my first novel and want to reiterate my thanks to everyone who has helped to make this book happen.

Miigwech!

RESOURCES

Culturally Safe Resources in Canada

We Matter is an Indigenous youth-led movement that has videos, toolkits, and resources for Indigenous youth in all provinces and territories. Find them at wemattercampaign.org.

The **Hope for Wellness Help Line** is a 24/7 national helpline for Indigenous people who are experiencing distress, dealing with traumas, or just need to talk. Call 1-855-242-3310 or chat online at hopeforwellness.ca. Help is available in French, English, Anishinaabemowin, Cree, and Inuktitut.

Talk 4 Healing is a helpline for Indigenous women and girls in Ontario. Call 1-855-554-HEAL 24/7 or chat online at talk4healing.com for help with crisis, cultural supports, and healing.

KUU-US Crisis Line (BC) is reachable at 1-800-588-8717 and available 24/7. It offers culturally safe supports for times of crisis, dealing with addictions, and addressing intergenerational trauma. The youth line is 1-250-723-2040. Find them online at kuu-uscrisisline.com.

The **Nunavut Kamatsiaqtut Helpline** is available at 1-800-265-3333 if you just want to talk, are in crisis, or are worried about someone you care about. The service is available in English, French, and Inuktitut. Their website is nunavuthelpline.ca.

LGBT Youth Line is not a crisis line but is a youth-led LGBTQ2S+ resource. Text 1-647-694-4275 or head to youthline.ca to chat online.

Kids Help Phone is available 24/7 across Canada at 1-800-668-6868 or you can text 686868. Their website is kidshelpphone.ca.

Culturally Safe Resources in the United States

The **National Suicide Prevention Lifeline** is available 24/7 at 1-800-273-8255. They have Indigenous-specific resources at suicidepreventionlifeline.org and are a safe space for LGBTQ2S+ callers.

The **Crisis Text Line** is also available 24/7. If you're in crisis, text HOME to 741741 to contact a counselor for free. You can text from the U.S. or Canada, or message them on Facebook. Their website is crisistextline.org.

Teen Line supports teens in crisis, those with mental health needs, or those who just want to talk about problems with someone other than friends and parents. Call 1-800-TLC-TEEN (1-800-852-8336) or text 839863. Find out more on their website at teenlineonline.org.

We R Native is an online resource for Indigenous youth in the U.S. that includes cultural resources, sexuality resources, resources for suicide prevention, and more. Text 9779 to follow them, or go to wernative.org for more info.

TrevorLifeline is a crisis line which helps LGBTQ2S+ youth. Call 1-866-488-7386, text START to 678678, or chat online at thetrevorproject.org.

Strong Hearts Helpline offers support for Indigenous people in the U.S. who've experienced gender-based or sexual violence. Call 1-844-762-8483 or chat online at strongheartshelpline.org.

You Are Not Alone Network lists crisis lines for many tribes at youarenotalonenetwork.org.